D0776875

🍎 BOOK REVIEWS

Here's what people are saying:

Gordon's amazing experiences come to life in this fictionalized, first-person narrative based on a true story.

from McNAUGHTON BOOK SERVICE

The story is exciting. Anyone who loves adventure will be fascinated.

from LUCSON CITY SCHOOLS

JUST FOR BOYS™ *Presents*

The
Upside-Down Ship

Don L. Wulffson

Frontispiece by Tom Centola

Albert Whitman & Company, Niles, Illinois

This book is a presentation of **Just For Boys**™
Weekly Reader Books. Weekly Reader Books offers
book clubs for children from preschool through high school.
For further information write to: **Weekly Reader Books,**
4343 Equity Drive, Columbus, Ohio 43228.

Published by arrangement with
Albert Whitman & Company
Niles, Illinois.
Just For Boys and Weekly Reader are trademarks of
Field Publications.
Printed in the United States of America.

Library of Congress Cataloging-in-Publication Data

Wulffson, Don L.
    The upside-down ship.

    Summary: Describes the adventures of teen-aged Bruce
Gordon, who, following an Arctic shipwreck in 1757,
survived for six years in the ship's upside-down
carcass with a polar bear as his sole companion.
    1. Gordon, Bruce—Juvenile literature. 2. Survival
(after airplane accidents, shipwrecks, etc.)—Juvenile
literature. 3. Arctic regions—Juvenile literature.
[1. Gordon, Bruce. 2. Survival. 3. Arctic regions]
I. Title
G530.G5987W85 1986   919.8'04   86-5555
ISBN 0-8075-8346-4

For my daughters, Jennifer and Gwen

Contents

Prologue

The people of Aberdeen sometimes refer to me as "crazy old Bruce." They think I don't hear them, but I do. Actually, I don't mind a great deal what they call me. You see, I am happy just to be alive.

I am only twenty-six years of age. Still, I know why they see me as old. I walk with a bit of a limp, having lost some toes to frostbite. And to cover the scars on my face, put there by the claws of a giant polar bear, I wear my hair and beard quite long. Both are laced with strands of gray.

I also understand why many people think I'm a bit wrong in the head. Partly it is because I often talk to myself. This habit comes from having spent so great a while apart from human company. For so long, the only voice I heard was my own.

However, I think the prime cause people think me a bit crazy is the story I tell. It is the story of my six-year voyage inside a frozen, upside-down ship. Many do not believe the story. They think I made it up. Honestly I cannot blame them, for the story does indeed seem peculiar, even impossible.

This is the story I will now put in writing for you. You may find it incredible, and sometimes frightening. But I swear that every word is true. I swear this on the Holy Bible.

1

I Dream of Adventures

I was born with a caul, a membrane enclosing the head, in the year 1740 in Aberdeen, Scotland. Those born with the caul, as tradition has it, can never drown. Later I would find this to be true.

Home was a poor farm near the sea. There my dear mother and my older brothers, Sean and Ted, raised turnips, rye, and potatoes. Dad, by the time I was a year, was dead of the white plague and resting in his grave at Loch Kinord. Still, Mother and my two brothers made enough to get by.

As a boy, I was a daydreamer, bored with everyday life and yearning for adventure. But others did not see this part of me. They saw me only as a lazy, sometimes belligerent fellow. Except for tending to the animals, I had little use for farming. Quite often I would shirk my chores. Many a day passed when my brothers would be digging spuds or engaged in some similar chore, and I would be off with other lads, fishing or seeing what sort of mischief I could get into.

Sean and Ted would complain to Mother about my behavior. Though she would not excuse my ways, she was also not very harsh with me, I being the youngest. This seeming favoritism, and my continued lack of responsibility, angered my brothers greatly. Sometimes they would seek me out when I was alone and far from Mother's protection. Then they would cuff me about. But I was not at all puny, and I saw no reason to take such treatment. I would lash back at them with my fists. Often I would take a beating; sometimes I would give one. Regardless of the outcome of these confrontations, my selfish ways did not change.

At school I was not much better. I considered myself to be very bright; the lessons, I thought, were beneath me, for all of the material seemed very childish and dull. Always my mind would wander. Hour after hour I would sit at my desk in the Deeside School, staring out the window at the docks and boundless sea beyond, dreaming of better places and better things. I dreamed of ships and pirates, of strange islands and buried treasure, and of violent battles from which I always emerged the victor and hero. As can easily be understood, my marks in school were poor and my comportment was worse yet. Rare was the week I was not disciplined for some infraction of the rules.

"What am I going to do with you, Bruce Gordon?" I can still hear my poor mother saying this. I can still feel her arms about me as she cajoled and begged me to change. Always I would promise to do better, knowing full well my resolutions were hollow and without any merit whatsoever.

As the years passed, however, even Mother began to lose patience with me. A painful distance grew between us, and I realized I must take stock of myself. I had almost come of age, and it was time I made some changes for the better, if only to save my mother from a broken heart. I must prove my love for her by setting my sight on some worthwhile occupation. But what? I was not fit to be apprenticed to any trade, and I had long ago learned to hate the fields.

"I am going to sea, Mother," I announced one day. "Every shilling I earn I will bring home to you. I will be a fine sailor. I know I will."

Mother wept a little when I told her. Though I was seventeen, I was still her youngest. The prospect of me being off somewhere on the high seas, away from home for months, even years, troubled her greatly. Nevertheless, being the good woman she was, she put her fears aside and gave me her blessing. I could see she was relieved and proud that I had at last determined to do something with my life.

2

I Go to Sea

The *Anne Forbes* was, to my boyish mind, a grand ship. A whaler, she was tri-masted and flat of stern. She was 186 feet on the deck, 52 feet in the beam. By any standards, she was large for a whaler. Her building had been done to the personal specifications of her captain and owner, a crusty Englishman by the name of Emmet Hughes. It was said of him that he was fearless, but that he loved his rum too much and his men too little.

It was on the *Anne Forbes*, on May 2, 1757, that I sailed from the port of Aberdeen for the Greenland whaling grounds. Though a lowly deckhand, I stood proudly as we broke sail and slipped gallantly into the open seas. On the crowded docks, shrunken by distance, stood Sean and Ted and my dear mother. She vigorously, they half-heartedly, waved to me. I waved back. And though I tried to smile, deep down I felt quite heartsick. I doubted that I should ever see any of them again.

The ship was no sooner out of port than the wind began to blow and the sea to rise in a frightful manner. And as

I had never been at sea before, I was horribly sick of body and terrified of mind. Of the *Forbes*'s complement of forty-nine, I seemed the worst off. I was ashamed of my sickness, and I cursed my stupidity at having wanted to become a sailor. I prayed earnestly to God to somehow return me to land.

My prayers went unanswered, and the storm increased. So high were the waves, I expected every one to swallow us up. And each time the ship slid down in the troughs between the great seas, I was certain we should never rise again. Helpless as a baby, I lay in my swaying hammock, waiting to die. Certainly, this was not the adventure I had dreamed of!

Not until mid-afternoon of the next day did the wind ease and the sea grow calmer. I ventured onto deck, and there I found, to my great relief, that my queasiness had all but passed. Though the *Anne Forbes* was still rolling heavily, I seemed now to be somewhat accustomed to it. Having survived the tempest, and now free of seasickness, I felt quite grand.

"Well, Bruce, a little less green around the gills today, I see," joked the boatswain, Jacob Estridsen. He clapped me on the shoulder. "A bit sick last night, were ye?"

"Aye, sir. Was a terrible storm."

Jacob ran a hand through curly gray hair. "A storm, you fool?" He laughed. "Do you call that a storm? It was nothing

14

at all. Give you a few months at sea, and you will think nothing of such a squall of wind as that!"

On our sixth day at sea I would find Jacob's words were all too true. On that day a terrible storm indeed arose. Mountains of water broke over us every few seconds and foaming torrents rolled about our decks. The mizzenmast snapped, and the sail was carried away like some great kite. Now I began to see fear and concern in the faces of the most hardened sailors. Some even dropped to their knees in prayer when the cry came from below that we had sprung a leak. This report was quickly followed by the news that there were three feet or more of water in the hold. I and all available hands were called to the pumps. Only the importance and monotony of this labor, I think, saved me from losing my mind to fear.

With reduced fury, this second storm continued for the next fifteen days. Then, on the evening of the 23d of May, the tempest suddenly and gloriously passed. The heavens filled with stars; the sea, seeming the color and consistency of the darkest ink, lapped softly at our hull.

The following morning dawned clear and blue and bright. The *Forbes* became alive with new spirit and energy as we all set about repairing the damage that had been done. The leak was patched with tar and shored with fresh timbers, and the hold was pumped clear of its sour-smelling water. The ship's carpenter set to work on the halved mizzen-

15

mast, and I was amazed at the cleverness with which it was repaired and refitted with a new sail. Sodden clothing and bedding was brought on deck, where it would dry in the sun and the gentle breeze.

I felt quite uplifted by all the activity and the fine weather. I felt, too, that I was now a true sailor. Twice I had faced storms, and twice I had survived them. I had gotten my sea legs; indeed, the rolling of the ship was almost comforting to me now. My mother, I was sure, would be proud of me. I had found a place where I belonged in this world, a place where I could hold my head up high. I was a sailor; I belonged at sea.

3

We Hunt the Mighty Whales

The days passed pleasantly. We entered the Greenland grounds, and ice and icebergs were everywhere, fore and aft. Though the sun shone brightly, the air was quite frigid.

Once we spotted an American whaler, the *Starbuck*. Captain Hughes hailed her, and for some time the ship sailed aport of us. Those aboard both vessels shouted greetings and news. The whales were plentiful and the hunting good, the Americans yelled to us. They wished us well; the *Starbuck* heeled hard abeam and went her way.

What the Americans said about the whales proved indeed to be true. The very next afternoon we spotted our first. Jacob Estridsen, standing watch on the foremast head, suddenly bellowed happily, "Hard astarboard. Thar she blows!"

There was a great commotion on deck. I ran to the bulwarks, and there, close under our lee, not forty fathoms off, a gigantic sperm whale plowed the emerald water. Its broad back glistened in the sun like some dark mirror, and a vapory jet arose from its head.

"Clear away the boats, boys!" cried Captain Hughes. The noise and the lowering of the boats must have alarmed the whale. No sooner had the whalers begun to row than the great creature lifted its tail in the air. Then it sank, its tail resembling a great tower being swallowed up.

Soon, however, more spouts were seen to leeward. The whaleboats went in pursuit. Pulling farther and farther away, they became almost invisible to those still on the *Forbes*. A great while passed. The men tired of watching. Then, suddenly, the boats rushed back into view. They were being dragged toward the ship by a harpooned whale. So close did the whale come to the *Anne Forbes*, it seemed about to ram the ship. A plume of vapor and water spouted from the hole atop the creature's head. It plunged down and disappeared from view; it had dived under the keel. The whaleboats went dead in the water. Everyone waited to see what would happen. Suddenly the lines snapped taut and the whale rose into view on the other side of the ship. Somehow the whaleboats were dragged along the side of the ship; then they floated free at the bow. The men in the boats prepared for another long ride, but the whale could take no more. Aimlessly, blindly, it went around the stern of the *Anne Forbes*, towing the boats behind. It made almost a full circuit. Then it stopped. It vomited blood, rolled onto its back, and died.

I was sickened but said nothing. I watched as the boats

towed the whale amidships. Then, following the lead of other deckhands, I dragged heavy chains along the deck. These were thrust, rattling, out of portholes. By these chains, the corpse was then moored to the ship.

All sail was taken in. The helm was lashed alee. I then expected the task of butchering to begin. But to my surprise, all hands were sent below to their bunks and hammocks till daylight. I asked Jacob about this.

"Cutting in is very hard work, lad. We'll be needing all our strength and a full day's light to do that task."

I looked over the side at the dead whale. One huge, humanlike eye seemed to be staring up at me. I felt sickened and guilty for having been party to the creature's death.

"A grand thing it is," said Jacob.

I nodded, not sure of what the man meant. Then I followed him belowdecks.

The morning dawned gray and cold, and it was an ugly sight that greeted my eyes when I gazed over the side at the chained carcass of the whale. To the spilled blood of the creature, sharks had been drawn like flies to rotting meat. From the sides and belly, they tore and gobbled great chunks. All about, the sea was a bloody, frothy caldron.

Hanging over the bulwarks, Nemsee, an East Indian, was spearing the sharks with a twenty-foot-long whaling spade. Again and again, he would strike the keen steel deep into the horrid creatures' skulls. And dying, the sharks would turn on each other, creating even more blood and madness.

I was greatly disturbed by the sight for, as you know, I had never been to sea before in my life. In my darkest dreams, I had never imagined such a scene. Too, there was no way I could have anticipated the events of the remainder of the day; the butchering of a whale, I was to find, was an ugly and devilish process.

The sharks having mostly dispersed or eaten one another by now, Mensee, Jacob, and another lad from Aberdeen, Andy MacDougal, leaped aboard the whale. Expertly they began cutting about the head. Finally it came apart from the body. Completely severed, it was hoisted aboard the ship and left swinging from the chocks astern.

At first I did not at all understand this. Why did they remove the head in such a fashion? In time I would learn that the tongue and brains were regarded as great delicacies. The French especially regarded them as such. Also, the head contained oils, these to be used for fuel and for candle-making. The ivory teeth were of perhaps the greatest value. From them would be fashioned all sorts of curious articles, including canes, umbrella stocks, and handles to riding whips.

After the head was removed, an enormous cutting tackle was lowered to the body. To this a great hook was attached. Nemsee and Jacob, armed with long spades, cut a deep hole in the skin, around which they carved a circular line. This completed, the hook was inserted into the hole. On deck, a windlass was turned and the oil-rich blubber was ripped off, then hoisted onto deck.

Dangling on its hook, the blubber was lowered through the main hatchway, down into the blubber room. It was to this hellish apartment that I was assigned. As each strip descended, we pulled it free. Then we coiled it into a blanketpiece. Thus rolled, it was barreled and stored in the belly of the ship.

The labor seemed endless. While we stored one strip, another would descend. Soon there was more than we could handle. Great piles of the blubber began to grow about us. There the surplus lay until time permitted us to attend to it.

My body ached and my hands and clothes were thick with grease when finally I ascended from the foul and stinking hold. My spirits already poor, I was further depressed to discover the day had passed and the sky was looming darkly.

Exhausted, I moved to the lee rail, gulping the clean evening air. I looked down, as I had that morning, expecting still to see the whale. Instead I beheld a peeled white carcass, stripped of its skin and blubber. It looked shapeless and very white, as though it had been bleached. And it was without its head. I turned to stern. I gazed upward at the great head that was still swinging aloft, creaking in its chains.

For a long while I pondered all this. Then sailors appeared and swung the head out over the sea. With a great splash, they let it drop. Then they pulled free the huge chains that bound the body to the ship. Separated, the head and body floated away, slowly vanishing into the gloom of night.

4

Terror!

There were more whales after that, a great many more.
There were twenty-three, by my count. Our holds became
heavy with their blubber. With each new kill, I grew more
and more hardened to my task in the blubber room. I did
it well and without thinking. To pass the time, often my
mates and I would sing as we worked.

It was now nearing the month of November, and we had
been almost six months at sea. Weighted down by her
catch, the *Anne Forbes* rode deeper and deeper in the water.
The temperature plunged. The icy seas roiled and heaved.
Clearly, the day was quickly approaching when we must
return home. More, it seemed to me that day had somehow
already passed. But still we sailed on, ever northward.
When, I kept asking myself, when would we begin the
journey back?

Upon returning home, I knew, I would not stay long—
only long enough to see my mother. I would give her my
earnings, as I had promised. For a while I would rest and
tell her about what I had done and seen. Then I would
book aboard another ship. For as the blood of whales was

on my hands, so too I felt it was now in my veins. Always, I would return to the sea and to the whale.

But for now I wondered only about returning to Aberdeen. And it was not I alone who wondered; many of my mates were asking the same question. All of us were troubled, for the sea about us was now beginning to freeze. Not a day would pass that I did not hear the others lament that the captain was taking us to our deaths. We were sailing too far north, it was said; with each passing day the danger from the floating ice and the mountainous bergs became greater. In the gloom of our quarters, many tales were told of ships that had become icebound, their crews and cargoes trapped for eternity in a frozen world.

Captain Hughes, however, seemed a man possessed. In the bowels of the *Anne Forbes* were enough ivory and blubber to make him well-off for many years to come. But, no, he wanted ever more whales, for reasons beyond my comprehension. Though fewer and fewer were spotted in these polar seas, and none were taken, he still pursued them with a vengeance.

One evening, passing aft of the captain's cabin, I heard him arguing with Jacob. The captain, by the slur of his speech, it seemed, was drunk.

"Turn back!" begged Jacob. "You will be the death of these men!"

Captain Hughes laughed. "We are now atop the North

Pole," he declared. "We can sail to China as easily as to Scotland!"

"Begging your pardon, but that is not true, sir."

"Not true, is it?"

There was a long moment of silence. Then I heard what I thought was the sound of liquor being poured into a tankard.

"Can you ignore the approach of colder weather?" asked Jacob. "Why, sir, do you refuse to head south? Everywhere there are ice floes. If a southerly wind should arise, I have no doubt the floes would imprison us."

"Leave me!" bellowed Hughes. "You are a coward! Leave me!"

What response Jacob made, I do not know. I hastened away. Quite unnerved, I made my way down to my quarters. Lying in my hammock, I kept thinking about what I had overheard. For a long while, I stared at the bulkhead. Now and then a bit of ice would bang against our hull, as if echoing Jacob's warning. Finally I dozed off. My sleep was fitful, filled with ugly dreams.

5

Into the Jaws of Death

For the next three days, as though to prove the captain's thinking correct, the sailing was quite fine. The sky was blue, the breeze steady; and the ice did not obstruct our passage. Midmorning of the fourth day, however, our situation changed dramatically. The heavens became leaden and overcast, and the wind, strong and erratic. Much more importantly, we found our vessel in the grip of a very powerful current. It was clear to all that we were drifting rapidly northward. This terrified us. Our lives, it seemed, were now out of control. The *Anne Forbes* was completely at the mercy of hellish elements.

These changes sobered even Captain Hughes. He ordered all sails set. He took the sun's altitude. He seemed troubled. He took it a second time. Suddenly he became panicky. He ordered the course be set due south. The *Forbes* came about, but the current was strong against her. She made little progress. Floes of ice, as if guided by some demon, closed in on all sides. Adding to the danger, a white fog began to form. Ghostlike on the deck, the captain barked orders with a vehemence born of fear.

Gradually the *Forbes* became completely surrounded by drifting ice. The floes, however, were fairly loose. Under short sail it was still possible to make some headway south.

We struggled onward in this way for over twenty-four hours. Then, suddenly, a very high and seemingly endless field of ice was spied ahead. The field was V-shaped. It looked like a pincer, rapidly closing on us. No escape seemed possible.

The captain slapped my head. "Up into the masthead, Gordon," he growled. "Keep a sharp eye or I'll have you kegged with the rest of the blubber!"

With great effort, I began climbing up the slick, cold mast. Inching slowly higher, I kept wondering what it was I could see that was not already obvious. We were ringed by ice. And ahead lay a solid world of the stuff. What could I do? Still, after some long time, I finally reached the masthead perch. Panting and terrified, I clung to the frozen wood. The ice-hard mainsail, buffeted by the wind, bounced me back and forth.

For a long while I stayed there, my body shaking and my teeth chattering. Feebly, I shouted warnings to the captain and the helmsman below. To me, my weak cries sounded foolish. From the masthead I could see no better than those on deck. Indeed, I could probably see less well; the fog seemed to be thicker in the shrouds than it was below.

Slowly the *Forbes* plowed toward the ever-closing prison of bergs. My mind began to wander. I knew I was going to die, but I also knew there was nothing I could do about it. I imagined being back home before a comforting fire. The thought of death did not pain me. The cold did. I wanted only to come down from the masthead and be warm again.

Suddenly there was a terrific impact. My mind snapped back to reality and I screamed. The unthinkable had happened! The *Forbes* had hit a berg! A great finger of ice had torn into her hull. She listed hard to port.

Below, men cried out and tumbled across the decks. The stern rose high in the air. The ship began to go down by the bow. Huge waves broke over her. Screaming, men were washed into the freezing sea. The *Forbes* shuddered. She rolled to port in a great swinging arc. Suddenly, though I was still holding on to the mast, my body was hanging free. I saw the sea below me; then I saw a sweep of ice. I tried to hold on. It was impossible. I cried out as my fingers slipped free, and I hurtled through space. A great whiteness rushed up at me. I slammed into it. My mind went blank.

I do not know how long I was unconscious. It must have been a considerable time, for when I opened my eyes a soft snow was falling on me. Indeed, I was almost covered by the flakes. My right side and shoulder ached, and my forehead also pained me. I touched my head; I pulled off a long spindle of frozen blood.

I looked about. I found that I was sitting on a huge flat chunk of ice. Perhaps it was the same berg that had crushed the hull of our ship? But what indeed, I asked myself, had become of the *Forbes?* And what had become of my mates? I both did—and did not—want to know.

In considerable pain, I crawled to the edge of the ice. I looked down at the sea and beheld the worst sight possible. The *Forbes* was gone, sunk to the bottom. Strewn about the ice were many bits of wreckage. Too, I spotted the forms of what appeared to be my comrades. None were moving, but I prayed to God that some were still alive.

On my belly, my head throbbing, I dragged myself forward. Then I sat up. Down a gently sloping ravine of ice I both slid and pushed myself to where the sea lapped against the berg. In trousers and jacket stiff as boards, I stood up and slowly made my way to each of my prone comrades. None still lived.

I was filled with great sorrow. I grieved, not only for my poor dead mates, but also for myself. By some strange quirk of fate I had been aloft when the *Forbes* hit the berg, and as the ship heeled over I was thrown clear of the sea and onto the ice. I looked up to God and asked why this had happened. Why had I been spared? Was it so that I might experience a strange and singular death? Was I being punished? Or, on the other hand, was I being rewarded? Was it somehow possible that I was meant to survive alone on the ice?

Amidst the wreckage there was a great piece of canvas. It was, it seemed to me, the greater part of the *Forbes*'s smashed jib. This, I decided, could be fashioned into some kind of shelter.

I pulled the sail onto the ice. Using bits of broken masts and spars, I began to erect a tent of sorts. My work, however, was cut short by a strange gurgling coming from the sea. Huge bubbles were rising and breaking on the surface. At first I thought it was some colossal whale rising for air. But then, to my dismay, a black, barnacled hull emerged in the spot. It was the *Forbes!* She had risen again, upside-down! With a great gurgling, she bobbed up high, settled down, then rose again, higher still.

For a long while I pondered what to do. I looked at the poor tent I had made. Then I gazed out at the *Forbes*. She seemed to me to be a sign from God. She had been sent to the surface as my salvation. I determined to reach her, or die in the attempt.

The ship, however, was still quite far from where I stood. I was separated from her by much ice and by a rapidly flowing polar sea.

I began picking my way across the floes. Luck seemed to be with me. I stepped and leaped from one chunk of ice to another. In all, they formed a perfect bridge. In very short time I reached the *Forbes*.

I pried a broken whaling spade from the ice. With it, I stabbed at the hull. Through all my efforts, however, I managed to make only a few dents in the wood. Exhausted, I lay back on the ice. Suddenly there was another great bubbling from the ship. Horrified, I watched as she gently glided off. I felt responsible, as if my efforts had driven her even farther out of my grasp.

Quite shortly, the *Forbes* again came to a halt. She wedged into a towering berg. Crushed ice now ringed her hull. She seemed to be stuck hard and fast. However, to reach her this time I would have to cross a very broad strip of water. The floes, though numerous, had great gulfs between them. Yet, I was determined to make a crossing.

The way was rife with danger. I climbed over small hillocks of ice as hard as rock. Then I came to other areas with the consistency of froth. There I slid into water over my head. I grabbed at floating islands of ice. I climbed on. As these would sink, I would dive forward onto others. Finally, frozen to the bone, I again reached the wreck.

On the port side there was no way to gain entry. Though a great hole had been rent there, this was partly submerged and wholly walled in by drifting ice. However, to starboard

I found a cabin window. With a kick, I smashed the icy panes. On my belly I crawled inside. The cabin was thinly sheeted with ice and was upside-down. A bunk, a stove, and a desk were still anchored by bolts above me. I was standing on the ceiling, looking up at the floor. Though the cabin was topsy-turvy, I quickly realized whose it was; it had belonged to our captain, Mr. Hughes.

I removed my frozen boots. Then I stomped about like a madman, trying to return some feeling to my nearly lifeless body. I found a bottle of the captain's rum. This I smashed open. I poured some of the contents on my frozen hands and feet. The rest I drank.

I then noticed a very large sea chest. I opened it, and to my surprise and delight found it was filled with nearly dry clothing. I shed my own, then proceeded to don as many items of apparel as I could manage. Because the captain was larger than I, his clothes fit me loosely, which enabled me to wear many layers of sweaters, trousers, and socks.

In a corner, I piled the rest of the captain's clothing. Into this odd bed, I inserted myself. A numb and giddy sensation took hold of me. I closed my eyes. And as I did, I realized I had drunk too much of the captain's rum. It was neither a pleasant nor an unpleasant feeling. Regardless, the spirits and my great weariness soon combined to overcome what little remaining energy I had. Momentarily I was fast asleep.

6

I Fashion a Strange Home for Myself

When I awoke I was disoriented. It took me a long moment to recall where I was and how I had gotten there. Too, my head and side ached from the fall I had taken, and I was terribly hungry and thirsty.

Eager to go exploring my strange new habitation, I fitted my feet into the captain's India rubber boots and made my way to the cabin's inner door. The door being upside-down, I had to reach up to the latch, and this had to be pushed in reverse. Though the latch moved, the door would not. A sheet of ice on the floor blocked its way.

I found a broadsword. With this I hacked at the ice. Finally I cleared the boards enough to gain access to a narrow companionway, this leading up to the ship's galley, larder, and general storage hold. Beyond the last of these, the way was blocked by slabs of foul dark ice.

In the larder I found food by the ton. There were beans and flour, pickles and yams, salted whale steak and bacon, and great varieties of other things. Only a little of it, it seemed, was spoiled. All, however, was frozen. But being terribly hungry, as I mentioned before, I was not about to let this factor stop me. I took some biscuits. I shredded them with a cleaver, then gathered up the pieces and put them in my mouth. I broke open another bottle of rum and took a sip. Gradually, the mixture turned soft, and I swallowed. In the same way, I consumed some beef jerky. At the time this seemed the finest meal I had ever eaten.

I made my way back down the companionway and reentered my compartment. I rested for a while. For a long time I sat upon the heap of clothing that had served me as a bed. I became suddenly frightened. What if the ship should heel over? What if she should plunge a second time to the bottom?

In great haste, I pulled myself out of the captain's cabin through the shattered window. I slid forward on the ice. Then, my eyes momentarily pained and blinded by the snow, I stood back and surveyed my situation.

The *Anne Forbes* was now totally locked in ice. She had become a part of the berg, and there seemed not the slightest danger of her going down. Too, the sea of floes I had traversed previously to reach the ship had during the night become a solid plain of ice. Across this plain, some twenty fathoms distant, could be seen odd mounds and heaps of wreckage, all mostly covered by a blanket of dazzling white snow. Forming a drooping, collapsed backdrop was the tent I had attempted to erect the day before. Also visible were the bodies of my poor dead companions, lying about like sleeping snowmen. Was the captain there? And what of Jacob? What had become of him? I did not want to approach that terrible scene.

I began walking around my ship inspecting her. She looked to me like a picture I had seen as a boy of Noah's Ark. My ark, however, rested not atop Mount Ararat, but instead in the side of some nameless mound of ice. Still, the notion occurred to me that Noah's boat had been his salvation; perhaps mine would be the same.

Walking around the *Forbes*, I scooped up a handful of snow, intending to eat it to slake my thirst. One taste of it and I spat it out; it was salty. I climbed to a higher ridge of ice. Here I found the snow and ice were untainted. I ate the stuff until I could stomach no more.

Following this high ridge, I was able to gain a view of the rest of the ship. Most of my attention was drawn to the port bow, for there a great hole had been torn. For some ten yards, the hull simply did not exist. Through this cavity the sea had rushed in, taking the *Forbes* down in a matter of minutes.

I returned to my cabin, determined to make it as livable as possible. First, from the larder and storage area I sought out provisions. I collected candles and lanterns, drums of oil, and kegs of fish and bacon. I hauled these to my cabin, then returned to gather up tools. I found a good ax and several saws, a hammer and nails, knives and whaling spades, chisels and lengths of chain. Truly, there was more than could be fit into my small cabin.

My next chore was to make my world seem right-side-up. Using hammer and chisel, I began to cut away the bolts that held the bunk and desk and stove over my head. Applying rope and tackle, I was able to lower these without causing much damage.

I moved the stove across the room. Adjusting the stovepipe, I made it fit through the broken pane. The arrangement needed testing. Into the stove I fed some scraps of wood. Then, after a bit of rummaging about, I located flint and steel and more of the captain's rum. Dousing the damp bits of wood with the alcohol, I had a hearty flame going in no time at all. The warmth soon filled the cabin. I removed some of my layers of clothing, having become overheated. Then I watched contentedly as the ice sheathing the walls of my cabin began to melt.

I next proceeded to fashion an outside door for myself. First I knocked out the remaining panes of glass from the window. Then from the galley I unhinged a cabinet door, and this I fitted into place over the missing panes. To the bottom of the door I attached a sturdy latch.

Feeling quite proud of myself, I began to tidy up my new home. Wet clothing and bedding were put near the stove to dry. For the desk and bed I found what I thought would be their most convenient location. Extra clothing and small tools were stored in the sea chest. My broadsword, whaling knives, and harpoons I hung on nails from the walls.

At such chores I worked for many hours. Tired but content with all I had accomplished, I prepared myself a meal on my stove. By candlelight I dined alone that night on a splendid meal of lentils, bacon, and yams.

7

I Am Attacked by a Bear

I passed the next several days in much the same way. I spent most of my time in my cabin making improvements, eating, and sleeping. I was much like a person in a cocoon. Though I was stranded in a cold, fearsome world, inside my cabin I could feel safe and at home. In there I could block from my mind how peculiar and dangerous my circumstances truly were. I was soon to learn, however, that this dormancy and oblivion could not continue forever.

One afternoon as I puttered about in my cabin, I heard a curious scraping sound coming from across the ice. There seemed to be many voices, and also the crunch of someone biting into a hard biscuit.

Had people somehow come for me? Was I to be rescued? These were my thoughts as I unlatched my newly made door and looked out onto the ice. I will never forget the horrid sight I saw. Near the wreckage piled some distance from the ship, many polar bears were prowling about. They were digging in the ice — digging up my dead comrades!

"Get away!" I screamed. "Get away from there!" My voice echoed and rolled across the frozen wastes. One great bear, sleek and plump and at least ten feet tall, turned and looked in my direction. Suddenly afraid, I pulled my door shut and latched it. Though I knew it was not in my power to change what was happening, I still felt like a coward. I wanted to do something. I wanted to stop the ugly, bloody feast that was going on. But there was nothing I could do, nothing but sit in misery as the horrid crunching continued out on the ice.

My guilt suddenly turned to sheer terror as I heard the sound of something approaching through the bowels of the ship. Seizing a boat hook in one hand and a harpoon in the other, I cautiously opened the door leading to the ship's galley. Slowly, I made my way up the companionway. My heart thumped in my chest. I stopped. I looked around. I saw nothing, heard nothing. Relaxing a bit, I passed through the galley and peered into the dark shambles beyond. I took another step. And suddenly it was there! A giant bear rose up out of the darkness of the wreckage. Roaring and with teeth bared, it lumbered toward me. Feebly, I heaved the boat hook at the creature, then rushed away. Gripping the harpoon tightly, I retreated to the companionway landing, then carefully backed down the icy, upside-down steps.

The narrow companionway worked to the bear's disadvantage. The walls pressed in on it, slowing its progress. Retreating, I kept the creature at bay, jabbing at it with the harpoon. For a moment the bear became trapped, its enormous body wedged between a wall and a broken timber.

39

Hefting the harpoon with both hands, I lunged at the beast and stabbed it. Blood spilled over its white fur. Roaring with rage, it backed away; then, as suddenly, it came at me again. The timber was knocked aside. The bear rose on its hind legs. One great paw arced down; my head and face, slashed to the bone, exploded with pain. Blood streamed into my eyes. Half-blinded, screaming at my tormentor, I drove the harpoon upward. It plunged deep into the bear's side. Pulling the weapon free, I continued the attack. Again and again I jabbed at the animal, driving it back. Then suddenly, on the icy stairs I lost my footing. I fell. The harpoon clattered from my hands, and I waited for the bear to pounce on me. But when I looked up I saw it fleeing, heading into the dark, icy bowels of the ship. It staggered and limped, leaving a trail of blood.

I looked down at a pool of my own blood. I, too, was gravely wounded. I put my hand to my slashed head and cheek. It came away red.

For a moment I felt triumphant in having fought off the bear. Indeed, I was so stimulated I scarcely felt any pain from the terrible gash I had received. Still, I knew I was in great peril. The bear had apparently entered the ship through the great hole in her smashed bow. And if one could make its way in, then so could more. Somehow I must barricade myself.

In the galley there was a large fire grate. I hauled this

to the entrance to the larder, then nailed it there to the bulwarks. I then used twine to lash knives, forks, and other sharp instruments to the grate, with their points outward.

Now totally exhausted and bleeding greatly, I made my way back down to my cabin. For medication, I daubed a bit of rum on my wound, bellowing at the pain. With a piece of shirt, I bandaged my face and head, then collapsed upon my bunk.

It was dark when I awoke, and I was in agony. The whole left side of my head seemed to be on fire. At the same time, I was shivering; the cabin was terribly cold. I tried to rise to light a fire, but I lacked the strength. Indeed, I did not feel well enough even to light a candle.

Then I heard the sounds again. The bears had come. And now they were in full force; there were many of them. I heard the grate rattle up in the dark of the galley, as though being shaken by the hands of angry prisoners. At any moment I expected all of them to break in upon me in my cabin. From above my bunk I pulled the broadsword from its nail and lay it across my chest, waiting.

But then the rattling stopped, and I heard the bears shuffling away. Miraculously, the grate must have held. For a long while there was silence. I thought—I prayed—they had gone away. Then suddenly my heart stood still. Now the great clawed creatures prowled the deck above; into the port hold, the bears had found their way! I heard the sound of wood clattering and being smashed. The creatures, I could tell, were at the kegs of blubber, rending them, tearing out the frozen blankets of flesh.

In the darkness, I lay in pain, staring into space. The beasts were everywhere in the ship. I knew they would somehow find their way into my refuge; my only question was how long it would take. Never in my life had I felt so piteously alone and afraid.

8

I Discover a Great Horror

For days I lay in a fevered delirium, drifting on the edge of consciousness. Sometimes I would see bears prowling my cabin, only to awaken and find I had been dreaming. The reverse would also happen. Once I dreamed I was standing before my stove, attempting to light it. But this time when I awoke I found it must actually have happened. Though I lay in my bunk and could not remember leaving it, the stove, I found, had been lit and was burning nicely.

The fever passed; my mind began to clear. Though still weak, I could prepare meals for myself, do small chores about the cabin, and take short walks out on the ice. Though red and swollen, my wounds were healing, scabbing over. In the captain's sea chest, I found a small mirror. I examined my face. A jagged patch of hair and scalp was missing, and three livid, parallel gashes extended from my left brow to my chin.

"Well, Bruce Gordon," I said to the face in the mirror, "you're not too pretty. But at least you're alive, you poor fool." For some reason I thought this terribly funny, and I laughed until the pain in my still-tender face could take no more.

Thank God, the bears had vanished and I had regained most of my strength; it seemed, therefore, a proper time to further explore my ship. On the floor of the cabin—my ceiling—there was a trapdoor. Standing on the sea chest, I was able to reach it. With a table knife I pushed aside the latch, and the door swung down on its hinges.

I pulled myself through the opening and discovered I was in the captain's storeroom. Holding a lantern high, I then entered the port hold. I studied the dark, tomblike compartment. The deck was heavily sheeted with ice and the walls were covered with hoarfrost nearly two inches thick. Strewn about were smashed blubber kegs, remnants of the bears' recent feast. Above, still racked and lashed, were countless more barrels of the stuff. Well above the reach of the animals, they had been left untouched.

In the dancing yellow glow of the lantern, I picked my way past broken cutting blocks, coils of frozen rope, and other debris. The place was ugly and frightening. It had once been beneath the sea. And, more recently, great beasts had roamed there. It was a place of death. The darkness seemed to close in on me, to suffocate me.

I quickened my pace and entered the main hold. Here, frosted windows lent some light, and I breathed more easily. Before me lay heaps of coal, scattered spars, timbers, rolls of canvas, and casks of fresh water—or, rather, fresh ice.

I continued on and found even greater treasures. There were knives and swords, even a crossbow. Muskets and pistols were racked in a hardwood cabinet. A closet yielded stacks of sealed kegs filled with gunpowder, packets of shot, and small boxes of flint and wadding.

I made several trips back to my cabin, hauling as many items as I could carry. Soon I was breathing heavily and feeling weak. I wondered if perhaps I was overtaxing my strength. I contemplated retiring to my bunk and sleeping the rest of the day. But my mind was wandering through the dark interior of the ship. I wanted to—had to—continue my explorations. Taking a deep breath, I made my way up to the forehold. I skirted piles of rubble and debris. I noticed that many of the hull's timbers looked folded, caved in. Feet-first, on my back, I lowered myself down an ice-covered companionway. I stood up. I was on a section of lopsided, twisted stairway. Stepping flat-footed, arms braced against ice-sheeted walls, I continued picking my way downward. A faint glow of light caught my attention. Making nothing of this at first, I continued on. My perspective changed, and as it did, I realized I could see more clearly into the bow. A shaft of light was streaming into the *Forbes* through the ragged hole the berg had rent in her. I studied the cavity for some time and determined that the next day I must somehow figure a way to close it to keep the bears out. A great undertaking! But I would do it, I decided.

"Wouldn't like me doing that, would you, you bloody savages!" I shouted, my voice echoing through the frozen hulk.

Silence followed. For a moment I felt foolish. Then I laughed. I felt giddy. All the pent-up fear and pain I had endured for so long suddenly welled up inside. Mocking the bears, I growled. I burst into another peal of laughter. Then my voice and my joy trailed away, replaced by deathly silence. Suddenly I was sobered. The peculiar hysteria of just a moment before was gone.

"I'll have to patch that bow," I said quietly to myself.

Feeling small and alone and afraid, I continued descending ice-sheeted, upside-down stairs. Stepping over a pile of rubble, I found myself entering the crew's quarters. I raised my lantern to the darkness. Dim light and twirling shadows danced over frozen walls. There were empty, upside-down bunks and rock-hard hammocks. My feet seemed to carry me on, against my will. I brushed against a frozen blanket, grabbed it, and stood still, staring ahead into the gloom. My eyes adjusted to the dark. I took another step, not sure of what I saw before me. It was a great slanting wall of ice. I held the lantern closer. Then I screamed.

In the ice were men! Hands reached out. Faces stared. Mouths were open, seeking air. When the *Forbes* had gone down, all had been thrown into a heap against the bulwark. Together they had drowned. Then the ship had risen.

Seawater trapped in the vessel had frozen. For eternity, the men were locked in an icy tomb.

"Oh, Lord!" I cried. "Lord, bless these men!" Retreating in horror, I stumbled and fell. I reached up, grabbed a frozen hammock, then fell again. Like an animal on all fours, I scrambled out from that place of darkness and death.

9

An Unexpected Visitor

For the next day and a half I remained in my cabin, a feeling of emptiness and dread gnawing at my soul. I stored new-found provisions; I cleaned and oiled pistols and muskets; I made my compartment as neat and clean as possible. I worked at a frantic pace, as though trying to erase from my mind the fact that close by, in the confines of my ship, men I had known lay twisted forever in frozen death. I could neither free them nor free myself of their awful presence. For their salvation and my own, I had only my prayers to offer, mumbling these as I worked.

When I could find no further chores with which to busy myself in my cabin, I gathered tools and made my way out onto the ice to the crushed bow of the *Forbes*. For a long while I studied the problem, discussing with myself how to go about patching the great cavity sufficiently to keep out bears. Returning to my cabin, I entered the captain's storeroom and port hold through the hatchway. There I gathered spars and timbers, stacks of canvas, and coils of rope. I then heaved these things to the ice below through a smashed window. The canvas and rope were frozen rock-hard. Outside on the ice, I set a small caldron of oil blazing. Over the flame I held the rope, then the sheets of canvas. As the material slowly thawed, droplets of water hissed and splattered in the burning oil.

The timbers were too thick to be nailed directly to the *Forbes*'s hull. I hefted them into place and lashed them with rope; then I pounded iron nails through the hemp and into the side of the ship to hold the beams securely in place. Slowly a clumsy wall began to rise. It grew to a height above which I could no longer hoist the heavy, cumbersome timbers. I leaned light planks and boards against the ship. I clambered up this wall, then pulled the boards to me. These I nailed to the hull. When finally the hole was mostly covered, I nailed two large sheets of canvas over the planking. Over the canvas I shoveled ice and snow. Soon, I knew, this would freeze solid.

Exhausted but quite pleased with myself, I stood back to admire my handiwork. "Not too bad," I told myself. "That should keep the beasts out."

Soft flakes of snow began to fall from a leaden sky. After gathering up my tools, I climbed a low bluff behind the *Forbes*'s bow. I took a last look at the job I had done, then headed back toward my cabin.

Suddenly I stopped in my tracks. Red-brown splotches trailed off through the snow. I knelt, touched the stuff, and smelled it. It seemed to be blood. Curious, I followed the trail. In some places, covered by fallen snow, the trail ended, only to reappear some distance ahead. I climbed a slope—

a stairway, really—of blocks of ice. On one of the steps there was a great smear of frozen blood, but beyond this, all was dazzling white snow. I made my way to the crest of the slope; through drifting flakes I peered down into a ravine. At its base there was a wide patch of red. And there was something else—an odd mound, seemingly human in its shape.

Moving carefully, I made my way down into the ravine. I stumbled along twisting, icy contours. Slowly, I made my way to the curious form in the snow. It was a polar bear, a female. She was dead, her eyes and mouth frozen open, her fur blanketed with sparkling crystals of ice and snow. I put a hand to a frozen stab wound in her shoulder, then to the wound in her side. Icicles of blood snapped off at my touch.

"So you died, did you?" I said, realizing the bear was the same one I had fought inside the *Forbes* several days before. It was apparent to me she had limped away, only to die a slow death on the ice.

Though dead, the bear was still a fearsome-looking creature. She weighed, I calculated, five to six hundred pounds. Her teeth were enormous, and her claws, though short, were razor-sharp. Looking at them, I touched the deep scars in my face. They were swollen and still very tender. Kneeling in the snow, I examined the creature more closely. As well as being terrifying, the bear was very beautiful. Her yellow-white coat was rich, full, and luxurious. Tiny ears and a thin, tapering face added to her beauty. She had tried to kill me and, in fact, had almost done so. Still, it troubled me to see the great beast lying there frozen, unmoving, without life.

"Well, the Lord have mercy on you," I said.

A frozen eye was fixed blankly on me. Lowering my head to ever-thickening flurries of snow, I rose from the beast. I made the sign of the cross, then turned away and began the slow trek back to the *Forbes*.

That night an Arctic blizzard raged. By candlelight I read from a Bible I'd found among the captain's things. Suddenly I was startled by an odd scratching noise outside the cabin. Then something came to my outside cabin door and bumped against it. Quite terrified, I grabbed a musket. I held my breath as a creature—a bear, I was sure—beat repeatedly on the door.

"Leave me!" I shouted. It was as though I was dismissing a person, sending away an unwanted visitor.

The pounding stopped. All was silent. For a long moment I stood transfixed, cradling my musket. Then I heard a faint, almost human cry. I did not know what to do, but I felt impelled to do more than just stand there. Cautiously I unlatched the door. My heart racing, I pointed my musket out into the night.

There, sitting in the dull shaft of light from the doorway, was a bear! For a moment I was frightened. Then, gradually, I realized how very small the creature was. It was not a giant beast like that which had attacked me; it was a tiny female cub. She looked terribly thin — half-starved, in fact.

For a long moment the two of us gazed at one another. I wondered how and why the creature had come to be there. All the other bears had vanished into the polar landscape, had probably retreated to frigid dens where they would pass the long, dark winter. Why was this one frail cub wandering about alone? Surely some disaster had befallen her, but what that might be, I could only guess.

"What a pitiful thing you are," I said.

The cub seemed to take this as an invitation. Warily, she made her way to my door. A bit alarmed, I stood back as she entered my cabin and began sniffing about.

"Well, make yourself right at home," I said, my nervousness turning to amused disbelief.

The cub looked at me inquisitively for a moment, then turned her attention to my table. She leaped upon it, scattering tableware to the ground with a great clatter. She found some biscuits and gobbled them greedily.

I laughed. "And by all means, help yourself to something to eat!"

Smiling, I made my way into the larder. I returned shortly with a keg of frozen blubber. With an ax I chopped it into small bits and set it out for her. As the cub ate, I watched her with fascination, still wondering what had brought her to my door.

Then a thought struck me. "Could it be it was your mother I killed?" I asked, my question directed more to myself than to the cub. I could not keep from seeing in my mind the carcass of the giant female I had found that morning in the ravine. It seemed likely that the little creature in my cabin had been her cub. Starving, she had wandered from the den and finally arrived at my cabin, attracted perhaps by the food and warmth and light.

Another question troubled me: If indeed this was the dead female's cub, then why had the mother been prowling about the ice, leaving her cub all alone? Had the sinking of the *Forbes* and the subsequent happenings wholly disrupted the bears' lives and caused them to behave in uncharacteristic ways? This, I concluded, must have been the case.

"I think it was your mother I killed," I said to the tiny bear. "It's best you don't understand that."

The cub looked up when I spoke, then returned to her meal and gulped down the last pieces of blubber. Done, she sat on her rump, looked up at me, and burped.

"Well, you're a pretty little girl, but your manners need tending to!" I chided her happily.

The little thing padded over to me and licked my hand.

A bit timidly, I petted her. I reflected on how curious it was that I had so recently fought a creature of this species to the death, and now I was welcoming its offspring into my home.

I do not recall my words exactly. But I said something such as this: "When I was a lad in Aberdeen, I had a bit of a crush on a pretty little girl named Nancy, Nancy McKinney. Cute as a button, she was. All the lads thought so. Being a bit shy, I never so much as said hello to her. Still, I was surely fond of the girl."

The cub yawned, curled into a ball, and closed her eyes.

I grinned. "It would seem, my dear, I am boring you." I stroked the animal's downy white head. "If it is agreeable to you, young lady, I think I will call you Nancy, after that girl from long ago in Aberdeen."

The cub opened one eye and closed it again.

I felt better than I had in a very great while. "Good night, dear Nancy," I said softly.

10
My World Breaks Apart

The Arctic winter settled over my world. Now the sky was forever black-gray and silent.

Nancy was growing; she was filling out, even getting a bit plump. Sometimes we would play and cavort about; however, it was her nature at this time to hibernate. She would sleep for days, then weeks, on end. Strangely, like her, I, too, became languorous, drifting off into peaceful sleeps for long periods, indifferent to the black, incredibly cold world outside.

Slowly, the skies began to brighten, the temperature to rise a bit. Spring arrived; Nancy and I, by degree, emerged from our long winter's slumber into a pleasant and lively new existence.

One of my first projects was to trim my hair and beard, which were very long and shaggy. I next proceeded to take a bath, which I did by sitting in a baker's bin filled with steaming water. This bath, though perhaps a rather funny one, was quite refreshing; it was my first since leaving Aberdeen so many months before, and I must admit I had begun to smell quite rank. My clothing I peeled away in layers and burned in my stove. Then I donned a holiday suit that had belonged to the late Captain Hughes.

Nancy continued to thrive, and in every way was a pure source of joy. She showed not the least disposition to abandon me. Rather, she seemed to look upon me as one of her own species — I think, as her father — and wanted to be with me wherever I might go. Often we went for strolls on the snow. At my bidding, she would walk upright, placing her paw on my arm like some fine young lady. We must have cut quite a figure. I was greatly amused and deeply pleased by it all.

In almost everything, Nancy would try to imitate me. When I talked to her, which was often, she would grumble and growl and move her mouth in the most curious way. She would even laugh with me. Eyes partly closed, grinning in her own odd fashion, she would emit the most peculiar sound. I can only describe it as being something on the order of the braying of a donkey. To her it was a laugh.

Each day the sun rose higher above the southern horizon. Swans in great number flew overhead, traveling north, their odd honking piercing my otherwise silent world. I perceived their presence as a dangerous omen, for it plainly meant that the polar seas beyond were beginning to open. Should my own ice field also disintegrate, it was possible that the *Forbes* would break free from the giant berg to which it was attached and quickly sink, taking Nancy and me with it to the bottom.

Using an ax and an adze, I hewed a stairway up the side of the ice mountain behind my ship. This provided me with quick access to the top, which became my observation post. From there I studied the seas all around for many days. Though I saw nothing to cause alarm, still I was troubled. Surely there must be something I could do to forestall the possibility of disaster.

The iceberg itself, I was sure, could never melt nor sink. I devised a plan. Not far below my observation post I began digging a cavern. I hollowed out one room, then, in the following days, added several more. One even had a chimney, fashioned from a sheet of tin.

To my ice house I lugged great quantities of supplies — food, blankets, muskets, and all else that might be needed should the seas begin to break up. Nancy enjoyed the place greatly, often romping from room to room as I worked at making minor changes and additions. Sometimes she would leap upon me, hug me, and together, rolling about, we would ruin every small improvement I had made during the course of a day's work.

Spring turned to summer. Though the days were very long and the temperature considerably higher than it had been, my world was still a frozen one, and there seemed no possibility of any sudden or dangerous change in my circumstances. Thus, as before, Nancy and I usually slept in our cabin in the *Forbes*. However, more for variety than precaution, we sometimes passed the brief Arctic nights in our house of ice. Nancy seemed to prefer this, for these new quarters were cooler and therefore naturally more comfortable for her.

One morning, bleary-eyed and perhaps more asleep than awake, I happened to glance out the entry to our ice house. I was dumbfounded. I thought I was dreaming. Before, all had been a solid plain of white. Now the sea to the north, to within a mile or so of my berg, was almost wholly free of ice! How this great change could have occurred during one night and without my being aware of it, I could not comprehend. Regardless, I was quite frightened by the unexpected change. I decided that Nancy and I should now remain at all times in or about our frozen apartments.

Nothing untoward happened for the next several days. Then one afternoon, as I walked about my observation platform, I was startled by a slight rocking motion of the iceberg. This strange tottering continued for some while. I watched as the berg twisted a degree or two to the west. Then, with a thunderous crackling, it separated from the great field of ice to the east, gradually creating a gap perhaps a mile long and at least a hundred yards in width. To the west and south, the berg was still anchored to the ice floe.

I hastened down the east-facing slope to the *Forbes* to

see how matters stood there. She was still on my side of the gap and firmly fixed to the berg. I breathed a great sigh of relief.

Nancy, meanwhile, had no interest in such matters. Her attention was drawn to the vast opening in the ice, the water there shining like some great green mirror. Happy as a child, she raced down to it and plunged in. Worried for her, I watched as she splashed about. I called to her. She seemed to smile, then dove beneath the surface. She was down so long I became frantic with worry. Over and over I shouted her name. Finally she reappeared, a large fish flapping about in her mouth. She scrambled out of the water and made her way to me. She dropped the fish at my feet. I praised her. Pleased with herself, she looked up at me like some great puppy. All that was missing was a wagging tail.

The act was repeated again and again. Strangely, Nancy did not usually eat the fish. Like a proud father, I clapped my hands in approval, praising her and petting her. Greatly pleased, she would drop onto her back and writhe in the snow, pawing at the sky.

The next weeks passed pleasantly, each day's activities usually topped off by a fine meal of fresh fish. Summer was waning; the air became a bit more chilled. With this in mind, and realizing it was a solid foundation of ice on which the *Forbes* rested, Nancy and I again began sleeping in my old cabin. I expected there to be no more changes in my situation.

I was terribly wrong. One afternoon, as I was reading my Bible, I noticed a slight shuddering. I opened my doorway and propped it on a stick of wood. I peered out. What I saw both terrified and fascinated me. The ice bordering the gap in the floe was gone.

What could have caused this? Had there been some great disturbance under the ice? Some freakish warm current that had caused this rapid melting? I stepped out of my doorway as I pondered these questions. As far as the eye could see, all was water. The berg was adrift. In my upside-down ship, I was once again sailing the polar seas.

11

Sailing Upside Down

For many weeks this strange voyage continued. I knew not where I was; I only knew I was sailing south. Several times I spotted mountains and fingers of land, but they were far away and well beyond my reach. From my lookout, I would watch as they passed.

Once I came so near land that I spotted a human being. It was a woman, I think, and she was dressed in furs. She was standing on shore, mutely watching me. I waved and called to her. Nancy, in imitation, bellowed loudly. The woman was frightened and vanished among some rocks.

At first I was greatly excited and uplifted by this contact. Who was this woman? Was she from some large tribe of people? Were there others also near? I pondered these questions, eagerly expecting to see more people. But as the days continued on and there was nothing of note to be seen, I began to despair. Unable to think of any new projects to occupy my time, I settled into a sedentary existence. On the ice outside my cabin, I placed a stool. There, wrapped in my warmest coat, I would pass the now shortening hours of daylight, dully contemplating the scenery. To fill this void, often I thought of home, especially of my mother. How my heart ached to see her again!

While I sat, Nancy hunted. Fat walruses occasionally

rested on the ledges of the berg. Too, seals would congregate there from time to time, replacing the usual quiet with their funny yelpings. Though Nancy was, as you know, very gentle with me, she was not so gentle with the seals. For hours, lying prone, her fur blending with the ice, she would watch them. When a hapless seal came near enough, she would pounce, and with a powerful swipe of her paw, end its life. As other seals slid terrified into the sea, Nancy would drag her catch away in her jaws. If I called to her, she would bring the carcass to me, which I would skin for its fur. If I did not call, she would consume her catch alone, this food being her favorite.

The berg continued on, silently plowing through turbulent, ice-flecked seas. Thick fogs descended, shrouding all the world. Winter was returning. The nights were growing longer, and soon unending hours of Arctic dark would again be upon us.

I passed most of my time in the cabin now, as did Nancy. Occasionally she would wait, much as a dog might do, by the door, bleating at me if I were not quick enough to let her out. Released, she would amble off into the snow, returning when she willed.

Nancy had by now grown to be many times her original size; she was at least six feet in length and weighed, I think, roughly three hundred pounds. This made it increasingly difficult for her to get through the outside doorway. Sometimes I would have to push on her rump to help her through. I set to fashioning a much larger and much sturdier door. After enlarging the opening with a plane and adze, I suspended the door from free-swinging hinges that allowed my big friend to come and go as she pleased.

Other than preparing meals, fetching kegs of blubber for Nancy from the hold, and the minor carpentry work I have just described, there was little for me to do. My only other worthwhile occupation was sewing the skins of seals into various items of apparel — things such as boots, jackets, and caps.

As winter descended, Nancy and I again began slumbering for very long periods. It was from one of these great lazy naps that I was roused one day by a rumbling noise. Looking out my doorway, I could see no change in the ocean. But as the sound continued, I decided to investigate.

Walking around the lower slopes of my berg, I soon discovered the source of the disturbance. To the west, a seemingly endless field of ice had formed. The massive berg, carried along by some strong undercurrent, was crushing through it with relentless violence. The ice rolled up against its sides, heaping higher and higher. Great walls of the stuff formed. The berg came to rest finally, fixed against this barrier. For the time being at least, my strange voyage was over; once again I was locked into a frozen landscape, somewhere on the polar seas.

12

Freezing!

For what I calculate to be more than three years, my stop-and-start journey continued in the same manner. During the warmer months my ship—wrong-side up and wholly fixed in ice—sailed the seas in a southerly direction. Then each winter the berg again was trapped by floes and frozen fast.

I sank deeper and deeper into a dark depression. I felt that I would soon lose my mind if I did not at least make an effort to escape my strange and frightening situation. I resolved to somehow reach land.

During the winter months, reaching land would not be difficult, for I would have only to cross the ice. But the fearsome cold at that time of year would surely kill me. Only in the summer, as it was when I first made my resolve, would it be warm enough to survive in the open. However, I was then—as always at this time of year—separated from land by a broad expanse of water.

What I needed was a boat. The *Forbes* had carried four whaleboats, hanging from davits off the main deck. But these had either been lost during the sinking of the ship or were pinned beneath the wreckage, crushed and frozen into the ice. For a time I entertained the notion of building a dory or skiff; however, I was not craftsman enough for such an undertaking. But a simple raft—that, I was certain, I could build.

On a ledge of ice near the sea I began work. I lashed several heavy timbers together, perhaps a dozen or more, and these I covered with a decking of oak planking, laid crosswise. For steering, I devised a tiller—a long paddle, really, held by a crude but sturdy rowlock. With some difficulty, I also erected a small mast and fashioned a sail. When at last the craft was completed, I stored provisions of every sort, bundling them in canvas and lashing them to the deck.

I was eager to set sail for land at once. But, as I've stated before, land, if visible at all, was usually far distant. In those perilous seas, I guessed I could make a crossing of only a couple of miles at best, and I hoped for a distance considerably less than this. I prayed earnestly for the berg to come close enough to land for me to attempt the crossing.

Shortly, I did indeed spot what appeared to be land—a massive, dark outline on the horizon—but I soon discovered this was nothing but a very large berg. Weeks passed, and I saw nothing. Then one afternoon on my observation point, I spotted a purplish mountainous landform to the southwest. It was no more than twenty miles distant, and I was running almost parallel to it. I studied the currents, hoping they would take me closer. Instead, cruelly, they swept me farther away, and the purple-gray outline of mountains disappeared wholly from view. I was bitterly disappointed. Only a few days later, however, a peninsula, an extension of the same land mass, I was sure, became visible directly ahead. With each passing hour it loomed larger — and the currents favored me, carrying my berg in a slow arc near the shoreline.

Filled with excitement, I raced down to my raft, Nancy ambling beside me, perhaps wondering at my behavior. Reaching the raft, I wanted to launch it at once. Instead, for a long while I studied the situation. It did indeed seem that the berg, as if guided by some unseen hand, was moving closer to land, closer to that moment when I could risk launching my raft toward the passing shore. The moment had come. I could not delay further.

The raft rested on spars, and over these rounded beams I had hoped to push it easily into the sea. It was not to be so. The spars had frozen to the ice, and likewise the raft to the spars. With an ax I severed the line that moored the vessel; I chopped away the ice and beat frantically on the frozen wood. The vessel slipped forward an inch or so, then stopped. It seemed I would never free the thing. I beat on it with the back of the ax. Despairing, exhausted, I sat down on the ice. I glared angrily at the raft and gave it a kick. It began to move. I kicked again. Slowly at first, then more quickly, it rolled over the spars. For a moment it hung over the lip of the ledge, then, with a soft splash, dropped partly into the sea, bow down. I made my way carefully onto the down-sloping vessel. On hands and knees, I pushed against the ice. I think more because of the currents than my weak efforts, the raft slid free. Rotating slowly, it bobbed out into the green water. I set the sail and called to Nancy. An instant later I was plowing through the water, my bear swimming gaily alongside.

I looked back at my berg, both saddened and excited to be leaving it. Regardless, there was no time for second thoughts now. I could allow myself to think only of the task at hand.

All seemed to be going well. Both the current and the wind moved me briskly. Within a few short minutes I had passed my berg and was headed on a favorable course toward land, no more than two miles distant. My heart was filled with joy. "We're going to make it!" I cried to Nancy. If she heard me, she seemed not to show it. She splashed alongside, her eyes fixed on the sweep of land ahead.

The wind strengthened. I loosened the sail, and for a long while my raft rose and fell easily over the water. Suddenly the breeze stiffened even more. The raft began heaving wildly; icy waves sloshed over it. I dropped all sail, deciding to rely solely on my tiller. This was sufficient for a time; then the currents seemed to change, and I could make no headway. I again raised the sail. That, I am sure, was my gravest error. Almost immediately the raft began lunging in a sideways direction. The large parcels on its deck shifted. One came apart; its contents tumbled into the sea. Crawling on my stomach, I grappled with the sail, trying a second time to lower it. I could not. My hands were stiff with the cold, and I could not manage the ropes. Waves broke over the port side, pummeling me. A great gust turned the craft almost on its end. I was knocked hard against the mast; I grabbed hold of it. There was a sickening sweeping motion. I saw the sail arc overhead. An instant later, I was in the freezing sea.

Choking, gasping, I slapped to the surface. Eyes stinging, I searched for my raft. Somehow righted again, it was racing away across the sea. It was already quite far away. Clearly there was no hope of reaching it.

Rising and falling in the swell, I saw rocky cliffs domed with snow and ice. Land was little more than a mile distant. But, at best, I was a poor swimmer. My body was numb with the cold, and almost every wave plowed me under. I scarcely had the strength to keep my head above water, let alone try to reach land.

I think I was near unconsciousness when I felt what I thought was a great piece of ice rising under me. I grabbed hold of it. There was a strange bleating sound. I pulled myself up and looped one frozen arm around Nancy's neck. I remember her looking round at me. Though I was terrified, fighting for life, there was no fear in the eyes that for a moment fixed on mine. I saw only fierce determination. As I rode through the rolling water, clutching this lovely creature's back, I felt oddly blissful. Vividly, I remember wondering at her concern for me. It was quite clear she knew I was in great peril—indeed, that I was near dying.

At first I had thought Nancy was taking me toward the peninsula, toward land. This was not the case. Gradually, I realized the land was growing more distant and the berg was rising into view.

Gasping for breath, I tried to pull myself onto a ridge of ice with no success. Then Nancy's great jaws locked onto the hood of my sealskin coat. She dragged me onto the berg. Somewhere at this juncture, I must have passed out. My next recollection is of a grainy tongue licking my face. I stood up. Confused, rocking from side to side, I tried to determine at what part of the berg I had landed and where my ship might lie. Though I could not be sure, it seemed that I was on the far side of the ice mountain, at a point directly opposite the wreck.

My sealskin boots and clothing were rapidly freezing. My body was like a solid block of ice; I could not close my hands, and I could not feel my feet. I saw Nancy waiting patiently for me ahead. Woodenly, I began to move toward her. She lumbered away at my approach. In great pain, I followed her trail.

I fell many times. On each occasion I was tempted to fall asleep on the ice and die. But Nancy would always lope back to me, bleating. Grabbing hold of her, I would struggle to my feet and hobble on.

How long I continued on in this way I do not remember. My legs, which I could no longer feel, seemed to move without me. An odd dreaminess settled over me. It was as though I were walking in my sleep. I recall at one point seeing the *Forbes* some distance away, but after that, I remember almost nothing. My next clear recollection is of moving along the icy sides of the wreck of my ship, desperately seeking my door.

I fell again when entering my cabin. Shivering uncontrollably, I curled into a ball. I wanted only to sleep. Nancy licked my face and bleated nervously. I believe somehow she knew I would die if I continued to lie there.

I forced myself to my feet. With great difficulty, I managed to build a fire in my stove. When more than an inch of solid ice had finally melted from my body and clothing, I cut off my boots and socks. A layer of skin peeled off my right foot. Both feet were still ice-cold and without feeling. I wrapped them with strips cut from a bed sheet. I ate some biscuits. I shed my clothing, then dressed again and made my way to my bunk.

I was feeling quite well when I drifted off to sleep, but I awakened in great pain. My toes throbbed fiercely. I forced myself to limp about the cabin, stomping sometimes, trying to restore life to my feet. This did little good. The pain only seemed to increase. I wrapped my feet in sealskin bags and tied these to my ankles with thongs of hide. I then again retired to my bunk.

During the course of the next few days the pain in my feet slowly abated. I thought I was improving. But one morning I noticed an unusual stench. I removed the sealskin bags, then the wrappings of cut linen. I was horrified. There were dark lines in my feet—especially in my right one—and these had split, showing red, bloodless cuts. Some of my toes were purple and bloated with infection.

I was in great fear that the poison in my feet would spread to the rest of my body. There was only one course of action I could take: the infected toes would have to be cut off. I sharpened a knife to a razor's edge, then proceeded to cut three toes from my right foot and two from my left. Ghastly though this might seem, it was not as painful as one might expect, for the toes were almost wholly without feeling. Regardless, the poison that had built up inside was in this way released.

My recuperation after this crude operation was remarkably swift. I bandaged the stumps daily, using salt and rum as ointments. I spent most of my time lying on my back in my bunk, my feet elevated by pillows. The condition of

71

my feet and remaining toes improved steadily, and my strength returned.

Once again I had escaped death. I felt deeply there must be some heavenly reason I had been spared. Many times I dropped to my knees in a prayer of thanks. And many times I hugged Nancy tightly, for this lovely animal had, to my mind, been the instrument of my salvation.

13

My Ship Goes on Without Me

It happened one morning that a dense fog arose as Nancy and I returned from a brief expedition across the ice. Winter was soon to be upon us, and I had wanted to get a bit of exercise and air. The outing proved a difficult one; due to the loss of my toes, it was only with great effort that I was able to make my way over the ice. Though my boots were tightly packed with bits of cloth where the toes had been, I was clumsy and fell often. It was with considerable relief that I headed back to the *Forbes* with Nancy.

Suddenly I heard a sound that filled me with disbelief. Someone had fired a gun! I stood petrified for some seconds; then I heard a second report. It seemed to have come somewhere from the west, but because of the fog I could see little, in that or any other direction.

I rushed to my cabin, returning an instant later with a musket and pistol. I fired the pistol into the air. There was an answering report, then silence.

My mind raced. Clearly, there were human beings about. But who were they? Where were they? Surely, my berg had come to rest on a frozen land mass; I was near some human habitation!

I hastened back into my cabin. Into a sealskin bag I

packed powder and shot, food and clothing. Soon Nancy and I were on our way, heading off in the direction from which I thought the shots had come and land might lie.

We traveled, I estimate, some two to three miles. Suddenly I noticed Nancy interested in something to my right. Making my way to where she sniffed about, I was astonished to find traces of blood on the snow and tracks appearing to have been made by the runners of sleds. I also saw many footprints, both of men and dogs.

With great excitement I began following this trail, Nancy trotting at my side. In an hour's time I found myself approaching a fog-shrouded ridge that seemed to mark the shoreline of a continent or island. Though I was tired, I kept on. I was certain I would soon find the people I pursued. I contemplated what it would be like, after so many years, to again be in the company of my own species.

Suddenly I stopped, rigid with horror. Everywhere about me the snow was smeared with great splotches of blood and gore. I approached what appeared to be a small bundle of fur. Examining this I discovered, with some revulsion, that I was looking at the remains of a dog. Not far from the body lay a broken musket and a spilled pouch of gunpowder.

Clearly there had been a furious battle here. Hunters and their dogs had come upon what must have been a bear. Shots had been fired. While the dog had been killed and devoured, the rest in the hunting party had made a hasty retreat.

I intended to do the same. The fog was again thickening and, I felt sure, the animal that had eaten the dog was not far away. Nancy and I had but one option, and that was to leave the area at once.

As fast as my clumsy feet could take me, I headed back in the direction of my ship. I felt both excitement and keen disappointment. That people existed in this frozen wilderness, and not so very far away, there was no doubt. But would I ever find them? I had come so close this time; I had felt so sure that I was, at long last, going to make contact with people. My failure to do so greatly increased my yearning and left me feeling more alone than ever.

Through the long winter days, I again began planning a pilgrimage across the ice in search of inhabited land. But this time I would prepare for an extended journey, properly equipping myself to confront the beasts and the cold alike.

When the days began to warm somewhat, I set about fashioning a small sled and loaded it with provisions of every kind: food and rum, extra shoes and clothing, lanterns and oil, and my warmest sealskin robes and blankets. Greatly in fear of encountering polar bears, I built racks for holding weapons on both sides of the sled. Within quick reach there would be a harpoon, ax, broadsword, and knife. There would also be three muskets and two pistols, each primed and ready in case of attack. In addition, as though these weapons were not enough, there would be the customary dagger and pistol in my belt and my best musket slung over my back.

After many days of work, all was finally ready. Excited, I eagerly tried out my new sled. In most ways it was perfect. It was sturdy, and the runners slid smoothly over both ice and snow. But the sled had one great flaw: it was too heavy. Pulling it behind me for only a half mile or so, I was completely exhausted. I was angry at myself, and on the verge of abandoning the contraption entirely.

Then the notion occurred to me that I might use Nancy to pull the sled. I fashioned a rope harness for her. As I slipped this over her neck and shoulders I was afraid she would be either unable or unwilling to perform the task I had conceived for her. Instead, she thought it great fun! She dashed off over the ice, dragging the sled behind her as though it weighed nothing! My joy soon turned to despair. At that speed, the sled bounced and jolted crazily. And suddenly it flipped into the air. It landed, with a crash, spilling its contents everywhere. Nancy stopped and looked back, seeming to wonder what had occurred behind her.

It took me a considerable time to repair my broken sled. I then set about to train Nancy. This to her was also fun. I made a leash. I walked beside her, tugging on it whenever she attempted to dash ahead. Sometimes she became irritable when I held her back. In time, however, she came to understand what I wished of her. She moved at a leisurely pace. I removed the leash and tested her without it. She continued to obey my commands and moved no faster than I desired.

I was ready to embark on my journey at once; it was crucial that I set out before the spring thaw. Anxious and excited, I made a last-minute check of my supplies and equipment. As I did so, Nancy frolicked about, making life miserable for a great fat walrus. I called her and, with some reluctance, she left the creature and ambled to me. I slipped the harness over her head and secured it.

I paused for a moment to look at my ship. For so very long it had been my home. I wondered if I should ever see it again; I wondered if I were making a great mistake in leaving it. I knew I was taking a great risk, that I could easily come to a terrible end, either freezing to death on the ice or being devoured by bears. But I had made my decision. God had presented me with an opportunity, and I must take advantage of it. My fate lay in His hands.

I yelled to Nancy, and we set off. The sled, with Nancy pulling, rumbled and rattled over the ice. Lumbering along behind on my bad feet, I kept pace as best I could. In some places the topmost layer of ice was thin and brittle, crackling as the runners of the sled passed over it. In other areas this layer had turned to water an inch or more deep. Ahead loomed the land, its dazzling whiteness standing in sharp contrast to the green-tinted ice over which Nancy and I made our way.

The journey across the ice took a long while, but I was so exhilarated, it seemed at the time to last only a few moments. I vividly recall the gleaming mass of land looming ahead. Nancy reached it first. She stopped and waited for me. Exhausted, I made my way to her. Plowing through high drifts, I suddenly tripped and fell face forward into the snow. My hand touched an outcropping of rock.

"It's land!" I yelled. "We're on land, Nancy!"

She looked at me quizzically, seeming to doubt my sanity.

In great spirits, I pressed on. We traveled a few miles across land that day, then made camp. Wrapped in sealskin blankets, using Nancy as a pillow, I passed the night on the snow. I slept soundly and well.

I awoke with the early dawn of the Arctic spring. It was a glorious thing to behold, filled with the most vivid colors. I watched as the sun changed from a disk of cold silver into one of warming orange. The sky turned from gray to blue, and long shadows retreated from a glistening landscape of endless ice and snow. It was all so vast and beautiful and empty. I said a prayer of thanks to the Lord and prayed that He keep Nancy and me safe.

We made good progress that first morning, covering many miles in a southerly direction. I stayed close to the shoreline, for it seemed to me that near the sea I was more likely to encounter people. Seal, walrus, and fish abounded there, and these would attract hunters and fishermen, I reasoned. Perhaps there might even be a whole community of persons who depended on the animals for their livelihoods.

By noontime I was quite tired. Still, on and on we plowed through the snow. The afternoon waned; I looked about for a place to camp. It was then I heard a muted, crackling sound some distance behind me. Feeling a strange sort of panic, I made my way to the lip of a bluff. I sat in the snow, looking down at the sea.

At first only small floes bobbed past in the currents. Then came ever larger slabs of ice. The field to the north, it was clear, had finally broken loose.

How long I sat in the snow, I cannot remember. However, I will never forget that moment when my gaze shifted. I looked up. Gliding past, no more than half a mile distant, was a large berg.

It was mine! Though miniaturized by distance, the broken hull of the *Forbes* was still discernible. I felt very anxious and depressed, for I was now stranded and wholly on my own. The great store of supplies in the wreck was forever beyond my reach; I had only my wits and a few relatively meager provisions on which to rely.

The current slowly carried my berg far out to sea. A frosty twilight settled over all. And still I sat, though the berg had become but a mere speck on the horizon. I envisioned the strange but comfortable home I had left. Closing my eyes, I saw my ship—my upside-down ship—sailing on forever without me.

14

The Earth Opens Up

I was now alone in a great wasteland. I knew not to where—
or to what—I was headed. I prayed to the Lord for
guidance. I prayed for deliverance from the dark feelings
that filled my soul.

Day after day Nancy and I trudged across the snow,
heading south. I expected at any moment to see signs of
human life. There were none.

Even though Nancy pulled the heavy sled and I carried very little, it was the habit of my friend to sometimes
advance far ahead of me. Keeping to my slow pace was hard
for her. At my bidding, she would do so. But there seemed
no point. Even when she moved beyond me, she did not
run wildly and upset the sled. And whenever I lagged too
far behind, she would simply stop and wait for me to catch
up.

It happened one day that Nancy was some hundred
yards ahead of me. I was making my way over a small hill.
Below, Nancy was moving easily across a wide plain of
snow. She paused and looked back at me. What occurred
next will forever remain etched in my memory. Nancy commenced ambling on. Suddenly the snow behind her seemed
to buckle and sink. In the next instant it collapsed com-

pletely, leaving a long black crevasse in its place. With the snow fell the sled. Nancy bellowed and roared. Stretched out on her belly, on the other side of the crevasse, she clawed at the snow. The sled was still harnessed to her. Slowly, its weight was pulling her to her death!

Screaming in horror, I ran down the hill and stumbled across the frozen plain. When I reached the crevasse, I cried out to Nancy. She bleated pitifully in response, sliding ever closer to the lip of the chasm.

I turned in circles, not knowing what to do. Somehow I had to free Nancy from the harness. But how could I reach her? The fissure in the snow was too long; there was not time enough to go around it. Perhaps I could jump across it? It seemed to be some six to eight feet wide. I backed away from it. My whole being filled with fear. I threw my musket and light pack to the ground. Then I ran at the gap. Crying out, I hurtled over black space.

I landed on the far lip of the crevasse but felt myself tottering backwards. I twisted, and flailing my arms, fell next to Nancy. Her eyes were filled with terror. Her forepaws clawed at the snow and ice. Yet still she slid backwards.

I struggled with the harness but could not move it. I grabbed my knife from my belt and sawed at the first rope tether. The strands snapped apart, and all at once the sled swung away, hanging now by only the one remaining tether. Nancy turned and faced the ravine. I reached for the other rope. As I did, the sled suddenly plunged straight down, the rope fluttering behind it. The harness had miraculously slipped from Nancy's neck and shoulders. Freed from the heavy weight of the sled, she scrambled to safety. Far below, the sled came apart against the ice. For a moment the pieces seemed to float in midair. Then they disappeared into the yawning darkness. Weak with exhaustion, I edged back from the crevasse and clutched Nancy. I was filled with an indescribable feeling of relief and elation. My Nancy was safe! I caressed her head. She was still trembling, her eyes wide and fearful.

My joy at having saved Nancy quickly turned to worry. I had lost my sled and most of my provisions. My food, my sealskin blankets, and most of my weapons lay scattered at the bottom of the crevasse. Still, I had my pistol. And then I remembered my pack and my musket, which I had shed in my desperate race to save Nancy.

I retrieved these, with some anxiety, by crossing the ravine at a point where it was still firmly bridged by rock-hard snow. Rummaging through my pack, I found a small pouch of shot, two more of gunpowder, and a small knife. There was a bit of jerky and some smoked fish. My Bible, flint and steel, and some odds and ends of clothing rounded out the lot. There was nothing more.

Still, I was alive. And as the greatest bounty of all, I had my friend. Together we had faced so many dangers,

I knew that somehow, with the Lord's blessing and guidance, we would survive whatever else might come our way.

I passed that night in a shallow pit, huddled close to Nancy. I wore every bit of extra clothing from my pack. But without my sealskin blankets, I was still terribly cold. I slept little. Rolled into a ball, I lay in misery, shivering from head to foot.

Though during this waning spring season the nights were not unusually long, it seemed an eternity before dawn would appear. But slowly, ever so slowly, the sky lightened and the sun rose. After eating a bit of jerky, I set off with Nancy in search of game. Our lives now depended almost wholly on what nature might provide.

As I have said before, Nancy was an unusual but quite skillful fisherman. We made our way down to the sea. Nancy plunged into the blue-green water, disappeared for a time, then eventually resurfaced with a good-sized fish in her mouth. This first fish I gave to her to eat. The second I gutted and cleaned. I wished dearly for some way of cooking it, but lacking fuel of any kind, I could not. I cut a thin sliver of flesh, put it gingerly into my mouth, and chewed. The taste was a bit rank but not altogether bad. I ate several more strips. The raw fish did not sit terribly well on my stomach, but it did not sicken me, as I had been afraid it might do. I was grateful for having found a means of sustaining myself.

As I continued to eat, I watched Nancy prowling about on an icy ledge along the shore. Something attracted her attention. She began sniffing about in one spot and moving in circles. Then, to my surprise, she started pounding on the spot with her forepaws! I thought she had gone mad. As I ran to investigate, she suddenly threw her whole weight forward. The frozen snow crumpled beneath her. I heard her roar as she fell into a small cavity of some kind. In the same instant came the frightened barking of a seal.

Already bloodied, the seal's head appeared. Nancy swiped at it with her paw and missed. The seal lumbered onto the ice, croaking and screeching furiously. Then it began to retreat, as if trying to lure Nancy away. Nancy followed and, in a flash, pounced on it. There was a terrible crack as its head was turned back on its body and its neck snapped. The seal was dead.

I heard a weak yelping sound coming from the hole in the snow and ice. I peered down. There was a bit of movement. I spotted a tiny white baby seal, half buried under snow, trying to free itself. I was fascinated. I was looking into a seal's den and birth lair. Somehow, Nancy had known the den was there. She had smelled it and smashed through the roof. It was now obvious to me that the adult she had killed was a female. The seal had given her life to save her baby.

As I pondered what had happened, Nancy brushed past

me, knocking me down. I yelled at her. Despite my protests, she snatched the baby and ravaged it. Momentarily, like its mother, it was dead. Its half-eaten body lay on the reddening snow. I yelled again. Nancy looked up proudly, then returned her attention to the carcass. I watched in disgust as she finished her meal. The scene sickened me. Though I had seen Nancy kill many times before, her devouring of this tiny infant bothered me deeply. I wondered how Nancy could relate to me in such a loving and human way and at the same time be able to attack her fellow creatures in the wild with such savagery. At that moment she seemed both very brutal and very contradictory to me.

Later that day I skinned the female seal. As I did, I had further cause for reflection. I needed the hide for warmth, for survival. With no feeling of guilt, I bloodied my hands in prying the hide from the flesh. Was I really any different from Nancy? Was I not capable of love and compassion one moment, of brutality the next? Indeed, who was I to pass judgment on my friend when we were so alike? We did not act out of malice, but out of instinct, out of the simple need to survive.

In this frame of mind, I continued hunting along the shore. At first, there was no sign of game. Then, to my surprise, I came upon an animal I had never seen before. It was a reindeer of some type, and it had become trapped in a very deep snowbank. I felled it with a single shot from my musket.

After cutting up the animal, I used its hide, and that of the seal, to make up two large parcels of fresh meat. These I carried, one at a time, into a frozen gorge. Being quite tired, and not convinced that further trekking across the landscape served any immediate purpose, I decided to settle for a few days in this place and devise some sort of habitation. With my knife, I dug an ice cave. On the floor I spread my two hides. These were not properly cured and smelled rather bad, but at least they would keep me warm.

I slept soundly that night, curled against Nancy and wrapped in the deerskin. But when I awoke, well past dawn, I was quite miserable. My clothing was damp and one hand lay in a puddle. Tiny streams dribbled down the side of my cave, and some parts of the ceiling of soft ice near the entryway had collapsed during the night.

Pushing my way out of my compartment, I found myself looking into a blazing sun. There was a strangely warm breeze, and most everywhere the ice and snow had turned soft and slushy. In a few places small patches of earth and rock were visible. During the night, summer had arrived.

I was perplexed. My plans of the day before to settle in the area had gone awry. I had wanted only to hunt and fish, to replenish my strength and supplies. But now my ice house was worthless; it would have to be abandoned. My aimless wanderings must begin anew.

Wearily I rolled my fresh meat in pelts and lashed them to my pack. Then Nancy and I left the place and headed south. I had not gone far before my feet began to bother me terribly. Slush and icy water saturated my boots. The stumps of my missing toes throbbed, sending sharp pains up both my legs. I had to rest.

Looking for a place to stop, I plodded on. Finally I came to the foot of a hill, snow-covered except for an outcropping of rock. The rock had been warmed by the sun. I removed my boots to let them dry, then fashioned crude stockings with strips cut from the deerskin. I ate the last of the dried fish from my pack, then lay back on the warm stone. The sun felt glorious. I closed my eyes. For a long while I lay in complete contentment, thinking of nothing at all.

Then I gasped. My heart racing, I sat up. I looked around. I could not see them, but they were there. Voices! I could hear human voices! Somewhere over the next rise, there were people!

15

In Human Company

I was filled with all sorts of odd fears. I was worried about my appearance. My hair was long, unkempt, and dirty; my beard was a gnarled shag. Would people think I was some sort of demon? Would I be understood when I talked? I was worried that I would make no sense, since for years I had talked only to myself and to the Lord and to Nancy. And what of Nancy, what would people think of her? Would they be frightened? Would they see her only as an animal to be killed?

This last thought worried me the most. I could not have anything happen to my dear Nancy. I cut some strips of sealskin and knotted them together, making a leash. I placed this about my bear's neck. Keeping a tight rein on her, I headed slowly over the low, snow-covered rise.

Anxiety turned to disappointment. I reached the peak of the hill and looked down. There was no one there! Had I been imagining things? Were the voices I had heard only in my own mind?

This seemed to be the case. I ascended another rise and again looked over a desolate field of white. I stopped to listen. I heard no more voices, in any direction. Forlorn, I started to trudge up another slope. Suddenly I saw a man walking down the hill toward me! Nancy tried to lunge from my grasp. She roared at him. The man retreated, leveling a musket at her! I raised my arms and planted myself in front of her. I put an arm about her neck, trying to show that she meant no harm, that she was tame. The man stared for a long while. Then he disappeared over the ridge.

I continued upward. I found myself following in the footprints left by the man. At the summit of the hill I stopped and looked down. Two men, clad in furs and armed with muskets, stared up at us from a short distance down the hill. They babbled at each other in a strange language, at the same time keeping their eyes trained in our direction. A dog ran back and forth, first rushing at Nancy, then quickly retreating. Nancy growled deeply, but she made no move. I held her leash firm and stroked her.

Meanwhile, the men had begun edging closer.

"Hello!" I called to them. My voice sounded strange. I pointed at Nancy. "She is like a dog," I said.

The shorter of the two men raised his musket. For a moment he scanned the area where Nancy and I stood. Then he sighted directly on me.

"Fool!" I cried. I aimed my own musket at the man's head. My finger moved uneasily near the trigger.

For what seemed an eternity, we remained fixed in one another's sights. Finally the taller man yelled at his companion. Slowly, the musket was lowered. The shorter man glowered at me, then spat into the snow.

I lowered my own weapon, took a step forward, and stopped. I raised my hand in a signal of peace. Stepping carefully, I then descended the hill. Nancy was skittish and tense as she followed me through the drifts. The dog, white as Nancy and long-furred, began to yap at us again. Nancy snarled. One of the men yelled at it. It dropped to its haunches, whining and looking about.

Near the bottom of the hill, we stopped. The taller man said something in the language I did not recognize. I forced a smile. I put my arm around Nancy's neck. The two men stared at us with a mixture of fear and wonderment.

"She will not hurt you," I said. "She is my friend, my pet."

The men looked at one another. Slowly at first, then with increasing excitement, they began jabbering. I watched in silence. A debate I could not begin to understand was going on. I watched the conversation. It became quite heated for a time. Then the two looked at me and nodded.

Both of the men were dark-skinned. Their faces were brown and oval-shaped, their noses flat. The taller of the two stepped forward and looked me in the eye. "England man?" he asked.

I was startled to hear these words, words I could understand. Though I was a Scotsman, I nodded yes.

The taller man said something I could not understand. I raised my hands in a gesture of futility.

"My name is Bruce Gordon," I said lamely.

The man tapped my chest. He pointed at a low range of hills, then at himself. "You follow," he said.

The shorter man pointed at Nancy and said something. His words meant nothing. But he was shaking his head. I understood him to mean he wanted no part of her.

I put my arm about Nancy and held up the leash, showing that she was under my control. I pointed at the hills beyond. "Follow," I said.

There was a brief argument. But it seemed the taller man had his way. With the dog and the other man at his heels, he headed off across the snow. The shorter of the two men looked back at us angrily, an ugly sneer on his face. Then he stomped away, trying to catch up with the taller man. For a while he trudged along beside the other. Then, little by little, he forced his way ahead. Nancy and I followed slowly, picking our way through the others' footsteps.

Attached to the men's boots were racket-shaped frames of wood fitted with crosspieces and crisscrossed with strips of hide. These prevented the two men from sinking in the snow, as I did. Thus, they moved much faster than I, and I had great difficulty keeping pace. Only the taller of the men seemed at all concerned with my plight. Now and then he would call his companion to a halt, then wait for Nancy and me to catch up.

In time, we came to an area where there was little snow.

It was quite a startling sight to me. Before us stretched a low, swampy plain. There were patches of moss and grass, and even a few tiny flowers poked their heads up out of the soil! This poor bit of plant life seemed truly beautiful to me, for I had not seen any for years, not since leaving Aberdeen.

I sat and rested as the men unstrapped the contraptions from their feet. I had plucked a miniature flower and was examining it as the taller man approached me. He pointed to himself. He said, "Nimauk," or something of the kind. I understood this to be his name.

"Bruce," I said, standing and pointing at myself.

He tried to form the word. "Uth," he managed to say. He touched me on the shoulder. "Uth," he repeated, smiling. Then he pointed at Nancy and shook his head. He said something to me and shrugged, a look of disbelief on his face.

It was clear Nimauk wondered at how a man and a polar bear could be companions. I put a finger in her mouth to show him how gentle she was. Very slowly, he reached out and touched her. I think I was as afraid as he; Nancy had never seen another human being before, and I did not know how she would react. At his touch, she looked up nervously. She sniffed at him, then nuzzled his hand. Nimauk smiled broadly and chuckled.

Some distance away, the other man looked on, scowling. Nimauk called to him. The man made a fist and shook it in our direction, shouting angrily. Then he turned his back on us.

What he had said, I did not know. But clearly he was very unhappy with Nimauk and wanted nothing to do with either Nancy or me. Nimauk attempted an explanation but gave up when I showed not the least bit of understanding.

With the other man setting the pace, striding ahead in sullen silence, we set off across the plain. In due time we reached another range of hills. Crossing this, we descended into a valley of smooth black rock, mud, and melting snow. At the end of this was a town of sorts, and beyond that a gray-green sweep of ocean.

The town was an odd place indeed. There were tents made of skins, shanties of sod, and long, low buildings of wood and stone. Everywhere I looked, I saw fresh hides stretched on poles to dry and cure and fish skewered on sticks being smoked over smoldering coals. The single unpaved street was a muddy, filthy quagmire. The raw stench of mold, human waste, and gutted fish and game filled the air.

Our arrival caused quite a commotion. People stopped their work and stared. Dogs snarled, edged forward, and had to be restrained by their masters. Eyes peered from windows and doorways. Children came running, shouting excitedly; adults approached more cautiously. I was interested to see that quite a number of the people were light-skinned, like myself.

I aroused a good deal of curiosity. But it was on Nancy that most of the attention was fixed. She was terribly nervous and kept pulling back on her leash. I tried to comfort and reassure her; she relaxed a bit.

A circle of people began to form about us. Nimauk stepped in front of me and began speaking to them. He was, I guessed, explaining what he knew of Nancy and me. There were exclamations of disbelief and wonderment from the crowd. And fear — there was much fear in the people's faces.

Nimauk put his hand on my shoulder. Then he addressed the crowd again. I heard the words "England man" and "Uth." All eyes turned in my direction. I felt both perplexed and embarrassed. It seemed something was expected of me, but I was not sure what. Something, perhaps, by way of introduction or demonstration? Everyone was waiting.

I forced a smile as I stepped to the middle of the circle. "Nancy," I said, patting my bear on the head. I pulled up on the leash; Nancy, wide-eyed and skittish, rose on her hind legs. Some in the crowd gasped and backed away. I turned the leash; my bear, still uneasy, walked in circles. I saw smiles; then there was nervous laughter and applause. I bowed. More applause. I pulled down on the leash; Nancy lowered herself and placed one huge paw on my shoulder. As the people laughed and clapped vigorously, we walked about arm-in-arm. I bowed again to the crowd, on the one hand feeling very pleased with our performance, on the other feeling a bit guilty at having exhibited my grand pet as though she were some sort of freakish clown.

A light-skinned man pushed his way through the assemblage. "How bloody good!" he exclaimed. "An Englishman, are you? A fine show, that was!"

I stared at him, dumbfounded.

He extended his hand. "Matthew Tennepot," he said.

I shook hands with the bearded, gap-toothed figure before me. "I am a Scotsman," I corrected him. "The name is Gordon, Bruce Gordon."

"Aye, Scottish!" he grinned. "But that is almost English, and good enough, to be sure!" He looked around. "All heathens and savages about here, as you can see. Not a bad lot really, for savages, that is. But the Danes! Now there's an odd lot!" He laughed heartily.

I studied the faces in the crowd. Every person was silent; all were watching.

Matthew Tennepot clapped me on the back. "There is a sturdy cabin behind my store. For storage, it is, and you are welcome to it, if you please. My place is the big one." He pointed somewhere over his shoulder. I glanced in that general direction, wondering which of the hovels he was indicating. "I'm the shopkeeper here. Exportin' an' im-portin'. Me place is the biggest in this godforsaken place."

I looked about. I did not know how to respond.

"A party!" the man exclaimed. "That would be the thing!" He turned to face the crowd. Smiling broadly, gesturing dramatically, he made an announcement in the strange tongue I had heard Nimauk use. There was a great cheer. "Tonight," said Tennepot to me, "there shall be a party in your honor. And a bloody grand time we shall have!"

16

Among Friends and Enemies

I was excited to be among my own species again. Still, I was deeply troubled. Though we had been greeted warmly enough by the townspeople, I had the strongest feeling that Nancy and I had entered a world in which we did not belong. We were used to the vastness and silence of the wild, not the close, noisy confines of a town. What was to become of my dear friend and me in such a place?

With these questions turning over and over in my mind, that afternoon I dozed in Matthew Tennepot's storage shed, Nancy at my side. The place was used to store hides and furs, and using some of these as a bed, I was warm and comfortable. I finally drifted into a deep sleep, only to be awakened by a heavy pounding. The door creaked open.

"They be waitin' on the guest of honor in the main ballroom." Tennepot chuckled, peeking in at me.

"Aye," I said sleepily. I smiled; Tennepot's joviality and boundless good cheer were quite irresistible.

"Time's a wastin', m'lord." Tennepot bowed.

I rose and made my way to Nancy. I petted her. She yawned, then struggled to her feet.

"A bit o' vittles for the lady," announced Tennepot. From

the folds of his great fur coat he pulled a fish he'd been hiding. With a laugh, he tossed it to Nancy.

As my pet attacked her snack, Tennepot and I made our way from the cabin, leaving Nancy. Tennepot bolted the heavy door, locking Nancy inside. I did not like leaving Nancy alone, but I had no choice.

In Tennepot's store there was every sort of thing for sale. There were bolts of cloth, muskets, bags of flour, coils of rope, tobacco, pots and pans — and so much more. Much of this had been pushed aside — to make room for all the people. It seemed the whole town must be in the long, low-roofed building. Women, some with babes in arms, hovered along one wall, eating and talking. Underfoot, a gaggle of children shouted and chortled with delight, playing some sort of game. An old man with a face of wrinkled brown leather sat cross-legged by a pot-bellied stove, watching the children and chewing and sucking on toothless gums. And everywhere, small groups of men had formed, eating, drinking, and babbling in strange tongues.

Tennepot disappeared for a moment, then returned with two brimming cups. "Some ale for ye, my boy."

I thanked him. We sat down on some boxes stacked near the stove. Many eyes had turned in our direction. The volume of chatter lowered for an instant; gradually it rose again as the people turned their attention back to their own concerns.

"What is this town called?" I asked.

"Kronenhavn," answered Tennepot. "And you be from Scotland, was it?"

"Aye, from Aberdeen."

Tennepot's eyes widened. "From Aberdeen to Kronen-havn—that's a far piece."

"Aye, Matthew. Sailed from there in 1757 aboard the whaler *Forbes*. She hit a berg and went down."

"Shipwrecked, you were, then!"

"That I was. And I do not even know what land this might be."

"It is called Greenland, but why they call it that is a bit of a joke, I think. There is little enough that is green about the place! They say the Danish called it that to get fools to settle here."

"And you are a settler?"

"That I may be," answered Tennepot, "but 'tis not by choice. You see, I am a prisoner here, as are all the Danes and other white scum."

"A prisoner?" I asked, quite puzzled.

Tennepot laughed. "A prisoner. Aye, that I am. And a long story, that is." He paused for a moment. "You see, the Norwegians and Danes begun a colony near this spot some hundred years ago or so. But there was a little war of sorts, and most of the settlers was killed by the bloody Eskimos. Bad times, they was, or so I've been told. And it all come about because of the influenza and the smallpox, which come with the dirty Danes and Norwegians. The Eskimos, they said it were a curse. All the whites, said them, was devils come up from the bottom of the sea, or some such nonsense."

"But you said you are a prisoner?"

"That I be, and a sailor like yourself, I was!" Tennepot took a long draught of his ale. "You see, after most was killed in Kronenhavn in the war, the Danes was needin' more to settle in the place, for the fur trade, mind ye. But there be, as can be imagined, few takers to come to such a cold and miserable place as this! So the Danes, they being a crafty bunch, they give thems who broke the laws a choice. Swing on the end of a rope or go to lovely Kronenhavn!" Tennepot glanced over his shoulder. "All the white folks here be thieves and murderers."

"But you are English, not a Dane."

"That I am, and proud to say so." He paused for a moment and stared into his cup. "My ship be docked one night in Copenhagen, and I get myself into a brawl with this big lout of a fool. A huge and stupid thing, he was. And only to defend myself, mind ye, I stabbed him with me knife. Died, he did. And here now am I."

"And you cannot leave?"

"When the ships come, the owners, they barter for the furs, but we are not allowed aboard. Forbidden, it is, and a hangin' offense, to boot."

"And about yourself?" asked Tennepot, as I pondered what he had said.

It took some time to tell Matthew Tennepot my strange story, and it was not easy, for the crowd was becoming increasingly rowdy and boisterous; at times I found myself almost shouting to be heard. Unmindful of all that was going on about him, Tennepot listened to me with great interest, now and then punctuating what I had to say with exclamations such as "amazin'!" and "blimey!" and "bloody good!" And when I had finished, he slapped his knee and bellowed, "Greatest yarn I've ever heard, and I've heard a few, to be sure!"

It was then I noticed Nimauk, standing not more than a few yards away. I called to him, and he ambled over, smiling warmly. He clapped me on the shoulder, and as he did, called out to a woman across the room.

A few moments later she and two young girls appeared with wooden plates, all heaping with food. These were passed to Nimauk, Tennepot, and myself, and we were handed small knives and odd two-pronged forks made of bone. I placed my plate on one of the boxes, studying it. The food was certainly nothing I recognized. In fact, it all looked quite horrible.

"What is this?" I asked Tennepot.

He chuckled. "They be Eskimo delicacies. That there," he said, pointing to some blubbery strips, "be the skin of the white whale. And the red meat be walrus liver. All o' it quite raw, as ye see, the way the savages like it."

"And that?" I asked, indicating a lumpish green mess that filled half the plate."

"Aye, that! That be the foulest food ever dreamed of. 'Tis the undigested contents o' a caribou's stomach. That's what it be." Tennepot grinned gleefully. "And there be hot water and seal blood for ye later, if that be yer desire!"

I looked at the food with disgust, then at Tennepot with horror.

"But you had better be eatin' it," he said seriously, "or you will offend 'em greatly."

Nimauk was already devouring his food with great contentment. Though I had not eaten in more than a day, I had no appetite. Still, not to offend my hosts, I nibbled at the contents of my plate, trying not to think of what I was eating.

Great shouts were rising from one side of the room. There, two Eskimos, stripped to the waist, were wrestling. Onlookers thronged about, laughing and yelling and cheering on their favorites.

After this match ended, another commenced. It was then I noticed Nimauk's sullen companion of that morning staring at me. Chewing a tough morsel of the whale skin, I asked Tennepot about the man.

"Oh, he's a bad sort, that one. Name's Sasut. A sneak

and a troublemaker, he is. His father Satunuk be the village *angatkug*."

"What is that?"

"A wizard, you might say. Witch doctor. It be believed his sort communicates with the dead and with spirits o' the sea, and such nonsense. An' him bein' Sasut's father gives Sasut a bit o' pull about these parts, if you catch me meanin'."

At the mention of Sasut's name, Nimauk turned to Tennepot and launched into a hushed but animated explanation. Tennepot nodded as the man spoke, now and then responding in the Eskimo tongue. Then he turned to me.

"Sasut's son was killed by a bear some two winters ago. He wants your bear and you out of here. Told Nimauk when they found you today the bear be a devil and would bring a curse upon the village."

I was about to respond to this when I noticed the room had suddenly become more quiet. Sasut was standing over me. He hissed something at me, then pointed across the room. He swaggered away. Folding his arms across his chest, he joined a group of companions. He was glowering at me, a mocking grin on his face. He said something under his breath. Those about him laughed.

"The goon has challenged you to wrestle," said Tennepot. "If ye do not accept the challenge, disgraced you'd be, and a laughingstock, that's for sure."

"I've lost all taste for fighting," I said, "but if this man wants a contest, then a contest he shall have." I rose to my feet.

"That's the spirit, lad!" said Tennepot.

The smile had faded from Sasut's face. In a wake of followers, he strode across the room, removing his fur-trimmed coat and rank shirt of sealskin as he went.

I followed, Tennepot and Nimauk at my side.

"'Tis the best two out of three," said Tennepot. "You must throw him to the ground twice, or he you."

I nodded in understanding, then stripped to the waist as Sasut had.

"Place both your hands on your opponent's shoulders," added Tennepot. "'Tis how each bout begins."

I nodded again and moved toward Sasut. He was shorter than I, but heavier, and powerfully built. His eyes were dark, narrow slits. Fat lips, arched in a sneer, revealed discolored, partly rotted teeth. I placed my hands on his shoulders while he placed his on mine.

An old man appeared at our side. He touched us both at the waist, then suddenly jumped aside and yelled something in the Eskimo tongue. Too late, I realized this was the signal to begin.

Sasut grabbed my right arm and in the same motion rammed his head into me and hefted me onto his shoulder. An instant later I was on the ground, flat on my back. Sasut was kneeling on my chest, grinning happily. A chorus of laughter greeted my ears.

Embarrassed and somewhat shaken, I rose to my feet. Taking a deep breath, I again met my competitor in the center of the yelling throng of spectators. And again the old man appeared and, touching us at the waist, cried out the words to begin.

This time I was ready. Sasut grabbed at my wrists, but with one blow I knocked both his arms upward. In a crouch, he circled before me. He rushed at my midsection. I sidestepped and planted a foot in front of him. He tripped and landed heavily on the rough-hewn wood floor.

"Bravo!" I heard Tennepot yell.

But now the final bout was to begin. Already I was greatly tired, and the clamor from the crowd was unnerving. Sasut hissed at me, his eyes filled with hatred. I placed my hands on his sweating shoulders and waited, every muscle in my body tensing. I felt the touch at the waist. Then came the signal to begin.

Sasut growled and rushed at me. His head slammed into my belly. I gasped for breath as he carried me backwards, my arms locked around his neck. We hit a wall and came to a hard stop against it. A thumb gouged at my eye, then fingers closed on my neck. I hit both the man's shoulders at once. He was knocked away; he turned 'round. Using my opponent's own strategy, I rushed at him low, butting my head against his ribs. He was knocked into the crowd, then was pushed back at me. His hands were at my face. I looped my arms about his midsection; his arms became a vice about my head. I turned my head slowly to one side; it slipped through sweating arms. I grabbed the man's thighs. Tottering under the weight of him, I rose up, hoisting him onto my shoulders. He screamed as I flipped him and sent him crashing to the wooden floor.

The crowd cheered and groaned and yelled with delight, all at the same time.

Panting mightily, I looked down at my opponent. He was on his side, holding a hand to his head. Blood streamed from his nose.

"Well done, my boy!" exclaimed Tennepot, looping an arm about my neck. "Well done, I say!"

I felt a bit dizzy and wholly drained of strength. "Thank you," I gasped.

Sasut was on all fours now. He yelled something at me, spat, then yelled something more. The room became silent. I stared at the man, wondering what he had said.

Tennepot and Nimauk guided me away. Nimauk put my coat about my shoulders.

"What was he saying?" I asked.

"All nonsense, it was," said Tennepot.

I stopped. "What was he saying?" I demanded.

Tennepot shrugged. "Bloke says he's going to kill you."

17
Murder!

I was a bit battered and sore the next day, but I was in a better frame of mind. Despite Sasut's threat, it seemed Nancy and I had found a home, at least for the time being. I ate a hearty breakfast, complete with tea and rolls smothered with marmalade, with Matthew Tennepot in his apartment. Then he and I, Nancy, Nimauk, and three others set off on a day's hunt.

The day began as a joyous and informative occasion. It ended in pain and tragedy.

An old woman and two young boys, all three with empty baskets made of reeds, followed us as we set off on foot. Shortly, we came to an icy stream that roiled out of the mountains. After traveling some distance along its banks, we came to a stop at a place where the waters narrowed. Built across the stream was a dam made of stones. Countless fish flopped about, trapped in the pond the dam created.

Nimauk and the others set about spearing the creatures with lances that had sharp, forklike ends. I wanted to join in the sport, but so did Nancy, which would have created havoc; thus, I had to hold her back and content myself with watching the others. After a fish was speared, it was pulled loose and dropped into one of the baskets that the old woman and the two boys carried. Soon these were filled to overflowing. Without a word, the threesome set off in the direction of the village.

Our outing commenced anew. For more than an hour we traveled due north, then turned inland and headed east. We came to an inlet, the water there thickly sheeted with ice. Tired and in considerable discomfort from my missing toes, I decided to rest. Tethering Nancy, I sat upon a low ridge and watched as the others headed down to the ice.

Nimauk crawled on his belly onto the ice. He stopped some distance from a small hole opening to seawater below. This, I knew from past experience, was a breathing hole for seals. A great while passed before anything happened. Then, suddenly, the head of a seal popped up. The creature looked about, disappeared for an instant, then reappeared a moment later and waddled out onto the ice. It closed its eyes and seemed to fall asleep. Nimauk inched closer. The seal awoke and looked right at the man. I expected Nimauk to remain motionless and silent. Instead, he began bobbing up and down, barking and honking and giving an extremely good imitation of a seal. He edged closer, continued his mimicry for a time, then fell silent. To my amazement, the seal seemed completely taken in by this act. Losing interest in the impostor, it turned its head toward the sun and dozed again. Nimauk suddenly rushed the animal. Too late, the seal realized its danger. Frantic, it lumbered toward the breathing hole. Nimauk's spear arced through the air and impaled the animal.

Nancy was excited by the spectacle and increasingly impatient to join in the hunt. I untethered her and we carefully made our way down the slope.

By the time we had reached the ice, Nimauk and another man were already skinning the seal, while Tennepot looked on.

"That was amazing," I exclaimed to Tennepot. "How could the seal be so easily fooled?"

"Don't know," he shrugged. "Can't figure why the critters fall for that sly old Eskimo trick, but fall for it they do."

I patted Nimauk on the back. "You make a fine seal," I told him, laughing. "Fine hunting!"

Tennepot translated. Nimauk looked at him and cackled, then turned and said something to me.

"The man thanks ye," said Tennepot.

After the seal had been skinned and butchered, I called Nancy and told Tennepot and the others to come with us. They followed as Nancy and I made our way to the edge of the ice. She immediately plunged into the sea.

"And what be you two up to?" exclaimed Tennepot.

"Showing off," I answered. "My bear and I have a few tricks of our own!"

A moment later Nancy pulled herself onto the ice and dropped a very large fish before me. I hugged her.

"Well, now ain't that somethin'! Fishes for ye! And like a proud father, you are. And yer girl, ain't she somethin'! A dear, she is."

"Aye," I smiled, patting her. "She's a dear."

This attention seemed to both please and excite Nancy. She dove into the sea again and again, never failing to return to the surface with a fish. Each catch brought her applause and added praise.

In good cheer, we all made our way back to town. Nimauk asked me to dine with him and his family that evening, an invitation I gratefully accepted.

In front of the shack behind Tennepot's store, I tethered Nancy. She seemed a bit on edge. I fed her several fish and a portion of the seal. "Enjoy your meal, girl," I said. She looked up at me. I gave her a pat, then made my way down to the hut where Nimauk and his family lived.

His home was a simple but happy place. There were two levels. The lower level was for cooking, socializing, and everyday activities. Above this was the sleeping area, a wooden platform supported by thick poles. The planking was carpeted with sealskin, and scattered about everywhere were piles of furs to be used as beds.

Two children peered down from the platform, giggling and chattering. Another sat in Nimauk's lap. He played

111

with the child as his wife prepared the meal. Through sign language plus a little of the Eskimo tongue and a little of English, we conversed as best we could, teaching each other a few words of the other's language.

Nimauk's wife was a very pretty woman. She was full of life and energy and seemed to never stop smiling. Using slivers of bone, she skewered squares of seal steak. Then, using a stone lamp that burned oil, she heated the meat. When the meat was warm—but not cooked—she passed pieces to Nimauk and me. The taste was foreign but not unpleasant.

"Good!" I exclaimed. I smacked my lips to convey my meaning.

Laughing a bit at my antics, the woman slipped a bit of the meat into her own mouth and, chewing, began preparing another dish.

There was a sudden loud pounding at the door. It flew open. "Come quick, boy!" yelled Tennepot, rushing into the room.

"What?" I blurted.

The man was out of breath. "Sasut," he gasped, "is rallyin' his father and his vile companions against you and your bear. Says she's a devil woman inside a bear's body and she'll bring death to the whole village. I saw them headed up from the bay. Says they're goin' to kill your Nancy, and that will kill you! That is how they plan to destroy you!"

"Nancy!" I cried. In the same instant I was out the door. With Tennepot and Nimauk at my heels, I ran up the mucky, foul street. Ahead, I could see a crowd gathering behind Tennepot's store.

"Sasut!" I screamed. Though I could not see him I knew he was there.

Suddenly there was the report of a musket. I pushed my way through the crowd. One man tried to stop me, but I knocked him aside.

And then I was in front of my shack behind Tennepot's store. And there was Nancy, on her hind legs, rearing back. Blood was streaming from a wound in her neck! An old man, who must have been Sasut's father, was dancing about in front of her, chanting in an odd, ominous way. And Sasut himself was being handed another musket. I lunged at him. Someone grabbed at me. An arm looped around my neck. I was thrown to the ground. I struggled free. I saw Sasut raise the musket and point it at Nancy. I leaped at him.

"No!" I screamed. I landed on the man's back. The musket roared. We fell together in a heap.

"You idiot! Beast!" I screamed.

Sasut spat at me as I struggled free of him. I stumbled toward Nancy. She lay on her side in the snow. I dropped to my knees, numb horror filling my whole being. Tears flooded my eyes.

I raised her head. She seemed to cough, to gag. I held

her to me and looked at her eyes. They were glazed, blank.

"Nancy!" I cried. "Nancy! Not you! Not you!"

She sighed. Her head fell limp in my hands. I stroked her face. "Please don't die, Nancy. Please don't die. Don't, Nancy, don't!"

But she was gone. My beautiful friend was gone. "No, God!" I cried. "No!" I hugged her head to mine. She was so silent. As I lowered her heavy head, my tears fell on her face.

And then I was filled with hate, with blind, murderous rage. I saw Sasut. He was grinning, backing away.

"Why?" I screamed. I leaped upon him. Over and over, I smashed my fist into his face. His rotted front teeth snapped. He spat one out. Then it seemed an army of men was pulling me away. I broke free and dove on him again. He seemed unconscious, but I didn't care; I continued hitting him.

Again I was pulled back. I no longer resisted; all my strength was gone. Then Tennepot was there, yelling at those holding me. They released their grip.

"I am so sorry, boy," said Tennepot. He put his arm around me.

I walked away from him. I knelt beside Nancy and lifted her head to my lap. "My beautiful girl," I cried, stroking her fur. "My beautiful girl."

18

Alone and Stranded Forever

With the help of my friends, I buried Nancy at the foot of a bleak and desolate hill. With her, some great part of me was buried. Inside, something was forever gone. I had never known such grief, such emptiness.

I prayed to God for strength. It did no good. I asked God how He could have let this horrible thing happen. Why, I asked, had He allowed the one thing I loved most to be taken from me? But there was no answer. There was only silence. I turned from God, even blamed Him for the loss of my Nancy. He, I felt, had betrayed me; she never had.

If I turned from God, I turned from humankind even more. People call animals beasts. But this is the opposite of the truth. It is people who are the beasts, not the innocent creatures of the wild. Animals kill only to live, to survive. Though humans, too, kill for this reason, they also kill out of malice and spite, driven by an evil unknown to other creatures.

For many days after Nancy's murder, I thought only of avenging her death. I wanted to kill Sasut. But would not doing so make me a beast like him? No, I wanted no part of murder.

During this time I stayed clear of all in the town, except Nimauk and Matthew Tennepot. Indeed, I think it was only their friendship that saved me from going mad. Their continued kindness helped me to realize there was still some good in the world.

Tennepot invited me to live with him in his small apartment. During the day I helped him about the store, cutting wood for the stove, cleaning up, and the like. When the townspeople came to barter furs and goods with him, they seemed to view me with both apprehension and sadness. Tennepot told me that most of the people felt bad about what had happened, and that only a very few had actually been party to the killing. More, Sasut and his father, by their deed, had lost the respect of a great many of the people.

I was not displeased to hear this. However, I still could not forgive the monster Sasut or his idiot father, nor could I really forgive the townspeople. They had stood by and watched the murder of Nancy without raising a hand in her defense.

As the weeks passed, my pain eased a bit. Still, I remained in a state of mourning, and for the most part was silent and bitter.

It was not until one afternoon in the waning summer season that I had reason for a renewal of spirit. As I was putting away some goods in Tennepot's store, I suddenly noticed a great deal of activity in the street. It seemed everyone was yelling and running in the same direction.

"What's happening, Matthew?" I asked.

Tennepot had run to the door and flung it open. "Why, a ship's come in, boy! A ship's come in!"

White sails billowed against a cold blue sky. On a northerly tack, the ship headed into the harbor. Its bow plunged again and again into the gray-green water as plumes of foam broke on either side of the bow. Sailors, made tiny by distance, hurried about the decks and climbed the rigging. All sail was taken in. The anchor was let loose, then plunged, with a great splash, into the sea. Fighting the anchor's pull, rising up and down on the swell, the vessel was dragged to a halt. It looked beautiful and filled the harbor with its wondrous presence.

Matthew Tennepot had spoken many times before of ships coming to Kronenhavn. Each, as he put it, "was like a gift from the angels." But they came neither often nor regularly. It was not uncommon, he said, for many years to pass between the departure of one ship and the arrival of another. I had certainly not expected to see one so soon.

On the crowded docks, I stood with Tennepot. He spoke of nothing but the goods the ship would bring. He was like a man possessed. His only thoughts were of his business and of trading his furs for the merchandise aboard the ship.

My thoughts were different. I could see Aberdeen. I could see my mother, see her face as I returned home. In tears, she would throw her arms about me, tell me she had

117

thought me dead. I would comfort her. I would tell her about all I had done, tell her about my strange adventure. And she would tell me about her own life, about all that had happened while I was gone. And I would feel good again. Once more, I would be with someone I loved. After so many years, I would be home again.

Two boats were launched from the vessel. Oars moved in unison, alternately dipping into the sea, then rising into the air, glistening with reflected sun. The coxswain shouted orders. Sailors pulled dripping oars over the gunwales and stowed them. Then they jumped into the lapping tide and pulled the boats onto shore. More men stepped from the boats. These were different. They were bound in chains and hand-irons. Behind followed yet a third breed of men, these carrying muskets. They yelled at the men in chains, prodding them with their weapons.

Tennepot counted. "Eight more Danes," he announced. "Eight more prisoners."

Looking defeated, the prisoners waited as keys were inserted and locks snapped open. They spoke in hushed tones to one another, rubbing sore wrists and watching as their guards returned to the boats. The boats were turned around and pushed off into the surf. The last of the guards jumped aboard. Sailors pulled against their oars; the boats bounced against the waves for a moment, rolled there, then moved beyond the surf and streaked smoothly away.

For a moment I was in a panic the ship would leave without me. Then, from the vessel, more boats were launched. There seemed to be a flotilla of them. Each was brimming with merchandise and goods. I relaxed. It was clear the ship was not about to depart, and that the business end of its venture had just begun. The crowd about me pressed forward. Voices babbled excitedly. All eyes were on the boats, bobbing in a bunch toward the beach.

"The furs—me furs!" exclaimed Tennepot. He hustled me back toward town. "Did well, I did, last time out." He gripped my elbow. "We must be first! First ones gets most o' the things!"

A bit dismayed but uncomplaining, I struggled to keep up as he hurried on.

His hands trembling, Tennepot unlocked the storage shed behind his store. He rummaged about in there for a long time. Then he came forth, hauling a great armload of seal pelts. He passed these to me and returned to the shed. I stood there holding the heavy stack of pelts, feeling like a fool. Finally, from the dark of the shed, Matthew once more staggered forward. He tottered beneath a mountainous stack of furs.

"Marten does well, but it be the ermine and sable them wants most," he gasped under his load. He staggered off down the muddy street.

I followed him, my feet squishing in the muck. My arms

became leaden under the weight I carried. The stack of sealskins reached to the tip of my nose. What if I should trip? What if I should drop Matthew's precious cargo into the filth of the street? I worried about this all the way back down to the docks. But more, I worried about my own predicament. It was vital I begin making arrangements for my transport home.

By the time we arrived at the docks, the boats were already on the beach and the trading was underway. A sealskin for a pot. Two hares for needle and thread. A musket for enough ermine to make some fancy lady a coat.

The haggling went on till sunset, then commenced again at dawn. By noon that next day I had made countless dozens of trips back and forth from the shed, carrying furs one way, trading goods the other. Finally, there was nothing left to be bartered.

"We did well, lad. Very well!" exclaimed Tennepot. On scraps of paper he was scribbling his transactions.

I put a hand on his shoulder. "Matthew?" I said.

"Aye," he mumbled, hardly looking up.

"I've done your bidding, my friend," I said. "But I've got things of my own on my mind. I have to return home, Matthew. It's all I live for."

"Aye, boy, so do we all. But you have forgotten."

"Forgotten what?"

For a moment he put his calculations aside. "Forgotten that we be only prisoners here."

I was stunned. "Not me!" I nearly shouted.

"That be true," Tennepot replied. He scratched at his beard. "But not to them, not to the Danes. To them we are all prisoners."

The boats were making ready to leave the shore.

"But I was shipwrecked. I'm a Scotsman, not a prisoner."

Tennepot ran gnarled fingers through greasy, graying hair. "Tell 'em, I would. I'd tell 'em you aren't one o' us. But understand, now, I don't speak their language." He shook his head. "I sees yer predicament, boy, and I wish I could be o' help to you, but 'tisn't any use. I cannot change what is."

"But I must leave, Matthew. I must!"

"Even should they understand who you be, wouldn't make no difference to 'em. Would not mean a hill o' beans to 'em, you ask me."

In torment, I paced away from Tennepot, then paced back again. I struggled to find the right words.

The man put his arm around my neck. "You have got to accept it, lad. You've got to understand."

"What?"

He looked me in the eye. "No one ever leaves this place. No one."

19

I Make a Desperate Bid for Freedom

For a long moment I stared at Tennepot. Slowly, his words sank in. "Never?" I asked. "I can never go home?"

"Not as I understand it, my friend. Not from here."

I looked over my shoulder. The last of the boats was being pushed from shore. "But I've got to try, Matthew," I shouted. "I've got to at least try!"

Tennepot shrugged his shoulders.

I dashed down the beach and ran splashing into the surf. "Wait!" I cried to the coxswain, a tall, balding man who was pushing the boat off. I tried to tell him I was not a prisoner, but he just shook his head and said something in Danish. He raised his hands palms upward, to show he didn't understand.

I raised one finger, asking for a minute. Then I waved frantically to Matthew, motioning him down to the beach. "But people speak Danish here, don't they?" I asked desperately.

"Oh, aye, many. Gustavus does, for one," he replied, pointing at a skinny blond man some ways away. "Want him?"

"Yes!" I exclaimed, my hopes rising.

Matthew called the man's name and waved him toward us. Then he dashed my hopes by adding confidingly, "But the problem is, he doesn't speak no English."

Gustavus emerged from the crowd. He looked first to Tennepot, then to me, his face a mask of confusion.

I glanced at the tall Dane holding the boat against the surf. Again, I raised one finger, asking for more time. The man looked annoyed, impatient.

I thought for a moment. "But you speak Eskimo," I said to Tennepot. "Do any of the Eskimos speak Danish?"

"Aye, many." He looked around. "Tinnuet does, for one," he said, motioning to a young-looking man standing near the dock.

By now a small crowd had gathered about us. There were puzzled looks on most of the faces. Many of the onlookers were speaking in undertones amongst themselves. They were puzzled and perhaps a little amused by the strange goings-on. Tennepot, Gustavus, and Tinnuet just stared at me, wondering what I had in mind.

I was nervous, but I tried to control myself. "Matthew," I began, "tell Tinnuet that I am a shipwrecked Scot, not a prisoner." I touched the Eskimo on the shoulder. "Then have him tell this to Gustavus. And Gustavus can tell the coxswain. It will work!"

"Aye, that's a plan, now! A brilliant bit o' thinking, it is," laughed Tennepot. "And I'll try me best for ye, lad."

He jabbered at Tinnuet in the Eskimo tongue. Tinnuet translated this to Gustavus. Then Gustavus confronted the tall coxswain. The man looked at me, sneered, and made a lengthy reply to Gustavus. This response was then passed from man to man, back to me. I watched anxiously. My translators seemed embarrassed, hesitant.

Tennepot looked at the ground and grimaced, then looked up. He put his hand on my wrist. "The fool says you are scum. Says you're just trying to trick them. His orders are to take no one from the beach. Sorry, lad, but I told ye."

The man shoved the boat farther out into the surf. As he climbed aboard with his comrades, he glanced back at me and laughed.

"Scum, am I?" I shouted. I broke away from Matthew and darted into the frigid water. I pulled my pistol from my belt and aimed it at the Danes in the boat. All sat frozen. I grabbed hold of the gunwale and pulled myself onto a heap of furs in the bow.

For a moment I felt rather foolish. I found myself lying on my back, pointing my pistol at half a dozen faces. "Row!" I ordered, pushing myself to a sitting position.

The men looked from me to the coxswain. I cocked the gun and gave my order again.

Angrily, the coxswain snapped an order. The men began to row.

It must have taken only a few minutes to reach the ship,

but it seemed like hours. My hands trembled. Faces stared at me. Finally, we bumped against the hull of the ship. I read the name written there in gold lettering: the *Briel*. I wondered what the word meant.

From above, ropes were lowered from davits. Oars were shipped, and the ropes were tied. Angry eyes continued watching me. Suddenly the boat was hoisted from the sea. For a few seconds we dangled in space. Then the boat swung inward and was lowered to the deck of the *Briel*.

I looked about. I saw a gray-whiskered man in a uniform of dark blue. He was, I was sure, an officer, probably the captain. I began to explain, to plead my case in a language they did not understand and with gestures that seemed to mean nothing to them. He shouted. Other men loomed near, pointing muskets at my head. I looked about for help, then dropped my pistol. A fist smashed into my face.

I licked blood from my lips. In a daze, I was pulled roughly from the boat and thrown to the deck. A foot lashed out at me. Again and again, I was kicked. My ribs exploded with pain. I was lifted by my arms and legs and carried across the deck, then down along a dark companionway and into the hold.

A door opened. I felt myself being heaved through the air. I cried out as I slammed against damp, rough planking. There was a deep laugh. I looked up as the door was slammed shut, leaving me in darkness.

20

I Await the Noose

I lay on my side, every bone in my body aching. The pain, and the taste of blood in my mouth, sickened me. I ran my tongue over a tooth that dangled by a thread of flesh. With thumb and forefinger, I plucked it from my gums and threw it away. Then I sat up and touched my hand to my throbbing head. The hand came away wet, sticky—with blood, I thought, but I couldn't be sure. The room, or cabin, into which I had been thrown was damp. And it was darker than night. I could not see my hand in front of my face to tell whether it was wet with blood or water.

I pulled myself to my hands and knees and began crawling. Reaching out, I felt a wall. For some distance, I moved along this. Then my shoulder smacked against something hard. A barrel. I moved sideways on my knees. And there were more barrels beside the first. They smelled of fish. It seemed I was in a storeroom of some kind.

There was no purpose in going farther. In misery, I sat down and leaned my head back against the barrels. For a long while I sat and thought. I now realized what a fool I had been to force my way aboard the ship. My rash actions had been doomed to failure. I had been told no one from Kronenhavn was allowed aboard the trading ships. It had been made clear I was no exception, and yet I had raised my pistol at the Danes. I had demanded to be taken home, demanded to be treated differently. I had been dense and unthinking. I had not anticipated the violent welcome I would receive from those aboard the *Briel*. But I should have.

I should have understood how they would respond to my violent act. In the frenzy of the moment, however, I had been blind, had given no real thought to what was to come. And for my offense, I would probably hang.

I could see my lifeless body dangling on the end of a rope. It was not a pleasant thought, but honestly, I cared very little. My life, it seemed, was already over. It had ended with the death of my beloved Nancy. And it had started to end when I had left the berg and my upside-down ship. I should have stayed aboard my strange vessel and been content to live that very unusual — but still peaceful — existence.

Why had I tried to escape? Why had I brought my beautiful bear among humans? That had been my gravest error, and it had cost Nancy her life. Had it really been Sasut who had murdered her? No, it had been me! Through my own stupidity, I had brought my friend to her death.

Then I had erred again. I had engaged in a criminal act to achieve my goal of returning home. Now, for this blunder, I was going to die.

With these thoughts turning about in my head, I closed my eyes and leaned back. I did not sleep or dream. Instead, almost in a trance, I continued to think. My worries kept going 'round and 'round inside my mind. I sought answers beyond my grasp.

I do not know how much time passed. It may have been minutes. It may have been hours, even a day. But suddenly a door was pushed open. And as the door swung, a triangle of light broadened to illuminate me. Silhouetted shapes appeared over me. I tried to rise. Strong arms reached for me and pulled me to my feet. Half-walking, half-carried, I was taken from the storeroom.

I was marched down a companionway and up a flight of steps to a door. One of the men knocked, then opened the door at the command of a muffled voice from within. I was trundled into a bright, spacious cabin. It was filled with people. For a moment I was confused. I saw Gustavus. And there was another familiar face—Tinnuet, the Eskimo who had tried to help me. Then Tennepot was standing before me! I blinked. I couldn't believe what I was seeing.

"Stupid Scotsman!" exclaimed Tennepot, grinning broadly. "A fine pickle yer in, lad!"

"Matthew!" I cried. I threw my arms about him and hugged him.

"A sorry sight you are, boy," Tennepot laughed. He

touched his hand to my swollen jaw. "A hard time you have had of it, I see. Beat you about, they did!"

I did not know what to say.

"Let us aboard, the good captain did, and it took a good bit o' doin'," said my friend. He pointed to the gray-whiskered man in blue serge seated behind a desk. It was the same man who had ordered my capture upon first coming to the *Briel*. "I could not leave ye. Swing you from a short rope they would, and still may. But begged 'em, we did, to come aboard, to save yer bloody, silly soul. We did that, boy, but the chances o' saving you be less than slim, I must let you know. And sorry I am to tell ye."

I put my arm around my friend. That was my way of thanking him, for I could find no words.

The captain rapped his knuckles on his desk. He looked directly at me and made a brief statement in Danish. Though I understood not a word, it was clear my trial had begun.

Behind the captain stood a very tall, balding man. It was the coxswain of the boat I had pirated, I realized. He pointed an accusing finger at me, all the while speaking to the whiskered captain behind the desk. It was clear he wanted the worst for me. As the man spoke, the captain scratched at his beard, looking off into space.

The coxswain came to the end of his argument. The cabin was filled with silence. A young-looking officer whose face I could not recollect began to speak. Seeming quite agitated, he pointed at the coxswain. From his manner and tone of voice he obviously had little respect for the man. The captain looked tiredly at the officer, and with a wave of his hand brought him to silence.

Now the captain looked at me and my friends. In Danish he asked a question.

"I only want to go home!" I blurted.

Tennepot squeezed my shoulder, silencing me. He turned to the Eskimo Tinnuet and spoke to the man at length. Tinnuet translated this to Gustavus.

Gustavus seemed nervous. He looked at Tinnuet, at me, and at Tennepot. Then slowly he approached the captain's desk.

I watched. I listened to the foreign words he spoke, wondering what he was saying. Then there was a heated conversation among the Danes, and at the same time among Tinnuet, Gustavus, and Tennepot. The cabin was filled with the babble of voices. I had no idea what was going on. I grew impatient and uneasy.

Suddenly Tennepot put both hands on my shoulders. He smiled. "The captain is inclined to believe your story. But you raised a weapon against his men," he explained. He pointed at the coxswain. "That one there be wantin' you hanged. Demands revenge, he does."

I tried to clear my mind. "Tell them that I am truly

sorry," I said. "I meant no harm. I was desperate. No one on shore would listen to me. I have been shipwrecked more than six years. I only want to return to my mother. I humbly beg the good captain for his mercy."

My words, translated from tongue to tongue, were passed back to the man behind the desk. He looked at me, and then gazed for a long moment at the ceiling. His brow was furrowed. He bit at a knuckle.

"Please, sir," I cried.

Tennepot looked at me sternly. He put a finger to his lips, demanding my silence. I hung my head. Then slowly, fearfully, I raised my gaze. I looked squarely at the bewhiskered captain.

The man began speaking. His eyes were fixed on me. I stood there frozen, listening to words I did not understand. The tall Dane behind him seemed angry. He paced and shook his head.

The captain glowered at him over his shoulder. The man clenched his jaw and made no more movement. The captain straightened himself and continued. Then he brought a fist down on his desk. He was finished. He had declared his sentence.

Gustavus turned to Tinnuet and explained what he had heard. The Eskimo nodded, then passed the same information to Tennepot. My friend was looking at the floor, listening carefully, his head bobbing up and down.

"What?" I demanded. "What?"

Tennepot wagged a finger at me to be quiet. He said something to Tinnuet in Eskimo. It was a question. The man answered, smiling all the while.

Tennepot said something else I couldn't understand.

The Eskimo made signs with his hands. Then he laughed and made the same signs again.

Tennepot turned to me, beaming.

"What?" I begged.

"You're free, lad!" he exclaimed. "The man has decided in yer favor. You're going home, lad, you're going home!"

21

Homecoming

The *Briel* traveled a northerly course along the eastern coast of Greenland. She made several stops, each time taking aboard furs in exchange for merchandise. She then sailed southwest, to Newfoundland. Her holds were filled with pelts of every kind — beaver, fox, ermine, mink, and seal. After taking on fresh supplies of food and water, the ship set sail across the Atlantic for Copenhagen.

I was uplifted by the prospect of at long last returning home, yet I was saddened to be leaving my dear friend, Tennepot, and those other good men who had come to my aid.

I was given duties of the lowest kind — swabbing the decks, emptying chamber pots, washing bowls and dishes. By many in the crew I was treated rudely and cruelly. Often I was laughed at or made the butt of some joke or prank. Being tripped, finding dead fish in my bunk, being challenged to fight — such things became a part of my daily routine.

I tried to ignore all of this. Inside, I seethed. But outwardly I showed no emotion. Never did I respond violently. In silence, alone with my pain, I endured my humiliation. Though I despised those who tormented me, I could not allow myself the satisfaction of avenging myself. Doing so would have given those men still ill-disposed toward me the opportunity of bringing new charges against me. For any violent response to this lowly baiting, I would probably swing at the end of a rope.

My only aim was to reach Copenhagen, and from there, my home. Each day, each moment, brought me closer. And I was not about to let a moment of rashness deny me my one remaining goal in life.

Finally, on November 3, 1764, we arrived at Copenhagen. From there—using the paltry wages I had earned aboard the *Briel* to pay my way—I shipped aboard a packet schooner headed for Scotland. Nine days later, my heart racing in my chest, we sailed into Aberdeen harbor. The sweeping vista of my homeland rose before me. There was the town, timeless and unchanged, and beyond it the rolling patchwork of fields, spotted with small houses of stone. The Presbyterian church still overlooked all, shaded by a stand of birch and oak fringing the cliffs above the sea. And nearby, dwarfed by the church, was the Deeside School, where I had caused so much mischief as a boy.

The schooner docked. Standing alone at the rail, I was overcome by the oddest feeling. Aberdeen—my home—looked so very strange after seven years away, not because it had changed in my absence, but because it had remained the same. It was as though I had never been gone.

Somehow, I had expected a warm welcome upon my return home. Instead, the experience was an empty, deflating one; no one knew or even greeted me. True, many eyes turned in my direction as I walked down the gangplank and debarked the schooner. But this was not occasioned by my unexpected and long overdue return home, for I went wholly unrecognized. Rather, the attention I received was due only to my odd appearance. I walked with a limp, and my hair and beard were long and shaggy and streaked with gray. The left side of my face was deeply scarred. On my feet I wore second-hand wooden clogs. My clothing was of sealskin, handmade and now worn and tattered.

I felt a bit embarrassed, and also disappointed. I was a stranger to the townspeople, and they to me. I wanted to tell them who I was, tell them of my ordeal, if only for the purpose of justifying my shabby and peculiar appearance.

Finally I spotted a face I recognized. It was the parson, Mr. McCole. At his elbow was a young lady, perhaps his daughter. I approached them.

"Sir," I said. "Do you remember me?"

The man tightened his grip on the girl's arm. They hurried away, glancing back at me apprehensively.

"I am Bruce, Bruce Gordon," I called after them.

If they heard me, they did not show it. They disappeared into the crowd.

Quite disturbed, I watched them go. I noticed a constable standing nearby, studying me. He was slapping a baton against his palm, and there was a condescending leer on his face. Then I noticed the others. Several townspeople had stopped and were staring at me. I felt self-conscious and somehow ashamed. A child was pointing at me, giggling. I stepped backward, trying, I think, to disappear.

"Look at the funny tramp!" the child lisped.

Many laughed.

I had endured so much to return to Aberdeen, but never had I expected a homecoming such as this! But what did it matter? I had made my return, not to see these people who belittled and laughed at me, but to see my mother. There was no evil in her and no stupidity. There was only love. On her, I could depend. It was for her, and her alone, that I had come back.

I pushed my way through the throng. Someone made a joke about my clothing, and there was more laughter.

I ignored all this and pushed ahead. Heading up a cobblestone street, I left the crowd behind. Two women, sitting on a doorstep and gossiping contentedly, paused for a moment to stare at my approach. I could feel — see — their heads turn as I passed. Other than the occasional attention my clothes received, my progress seemed to go unnoticed. I purposely picked the most quiet and empty parts of town through which to make my way. The cobblestone streets ended. I was on a rock-hard dirt path. I passed the Deeside School and headed inland. I knew the winding, rutted road well. As a boy, I had traveled it often. It led home.

A noonday sun beat down upon me. I seemed to be sweating from every pore, and I felt weak and giddy. But one foot followed another. I lumbered on, past familiar fields and familiar houses.

And then I stopped. There it was before me — our farm! For the most part it looked the same as the day I had left. Rye shimmered in the wind. Sheep bleated. The old farmhouse stood silhouetted against a blue sky. I was home. Thanks be to God, at long last I was home!

My heart was filled with joy. I leapt. I crashed into the rye. I scrambled through it and out of it, and hurried on aching feet toward the house. A man was emerging from a shed. It was my brother! It was Ted! In either hand he carried a bucket of slops for the pigs. A young girl, singing a song of sorts and hugging a doll, followed behind.

"Ted!" I shouted, limping toward him.

He stared in disbelief, then set the slop buckets on the ground.

"It is I! Bruce, your brother!"

He took one step toward me, then another. His eyes were wide. "But you are dead! Your ship was lost, they said! Is it really you?"

I stood before him. "Shipwrecked, we were. My shipmates are all dead, God bless 'em. I was the only man to survive. And back now, I am!"

"Shipwrecked?" he asked, scratching his head. I thought

he was going to ask me about my adventures. Instead he repeated, "But you are dead. Dead, you were."

"Aye, but back I am. And Mother? Where is Mother?"

Ted's face hardened. "Where is she? In the grave, she is. In the ground, beside Father, is our mother!"

"Dead?" Filled with dread and anguish, I asked the question.

"Aye, and thanks much to you," he said bitterly. "Died of a broken heart, she did, hearing of the loss of you, her favorite son."

I felt sick and weak. "Dead?" I asked again. I sat down on a chopping block. Closing my eyes, I fought the tears.

"Gone now three years, she has been. And Sean is in the Americas, seeking fame and fortune." He spat. "And good riddance!"

A door opened and a heavy-set woman peered out, wiping her hands on a cloth. "And who might that be?" she said crankily, an eyebrow raised in my direction.

"No one! Be off with ye, woman!"

The door closed. All was silent, save for the gentle chirping and twittering of some solitary bird, invisible in the branches of the oak towering over our dooryard. I studied the tree. It was a part of my earliest memory. I gazed up into the leafy branches. Fleeting visions of earlier, happier times passed before my eyes.

"Why are you crying, sir?" A hand touched my knee. I looked into the face of the little girl.

I patted her flaxen head and forced a smile. "For many things, little one," I said. I touched a freckle on her nose.

Ted pulled her away and turned her around. "Off with you! Be about your chores now, child!" he ordered.

The child looked back at me. "Goody-bye, sir," she said softly, and walked away. The tiny thing, her head lowered, trudged off toward the barn and disappeared into the ancient, sagging building.

Ted rocked back and forth nervously. He crossed his arms and looked down at me. He seemed worried, deep in thought. His eyes were fixed on mine. "Always the lazy one, you were," he said. "And done nothing with your life, by the looks of you."

I gazed up at him. There was so much I wanted to say to him. Instead, I looked down and said nothing.

"Done nothing," he scolded again.

When I still made no reply, he moved even nearer, seeming to puff up with self-worth. "Worked this stony farm all these years, I have. And now here you sit, a tramp come home from the seas! Look at ye!"

I studied my shabby clothes. They brought back a world of memories. I raised my head and fixed my gaze on my brother.

"Left the farm, you did." His brow was furrowed and

his eyes looked hard and calculating. "Left it, you and Sean did both." His face became a stone. "The place belongs to me now, and that is clear! No claim to it do you have, though you might be thinking you do."

"Aye, none," I replied, standing up. "That was your worry?"

He nodded, wary.

"I want no part of your farm. None of it belongs to me."

He looked suddenly relieved. He smiled. "But bein' your brother, some old clothes and a guinea or two I might let you have."

I wanted to laugh and to cry at the same time. I shook my head.

Ted's face reddened. "Not enough for ye? No? But not a shilling more shall you have from me!"

I was heartsick. "I want nothing from you, Ted," I said. "That is not why I am here."

"Nothing?" His face reddened even more. "Then nothing it shall be!" he snapped.

I stood up and wiped at a damp eye. I looked at my brother for a moment. "Good-bye, Ted," I said, then turned and walked away.

Epilogue

It is going on two years now since my return to Aberdeen.
For the first few months after coming home I worked on
the docks, loading and unloading cargo. My home, if it
could be called that, was a small room above a tavern.

Now and then, to those who cared to listen, I told the
story of my great adventure. Many people believed me; more
than a few, however, did not. The latter were inclined to
laugh, usually behind my back, and call me "crazy old
Bruce." To them, the story seemed too incredible to be true.

All in all, I felt much apart from my fellow man. I had
been wronged many times in the past, and now I was
generally scorned by society. Too, the many years I had
passed in the silence of the Arctic had changed me into
a quiet man, and it became my habit to want to be alone.
Thus, I felt very alienated, both because of my treatment
at the hands of others and because of my peculiar
experience.

Truly, I was a very bitter and very solitary man for quite
some time. But that is all behind me now. In the autumn
of '65 I met a fine woman, Beth MacKenzie. Beth is not
a handsome woman, but she is beautiful of spirit, and as
you know, that is the most important thing. On Christmas
Eve of last year we were wed. Together we built a small

cottage near the sea. There we raise sheep for their wool. And we have a great fine mutt of a dog. I call her Miss Forbes, after my ship.

Through Beth's love and kindness I have found renewed spirit and love of life. More, I have found an answer to my question of long ago: Why was I alone spared when all of my shipmates perished? I think perhaps it was that there be someone to tell this tale. More assuredly, it was that I might learn — and share with you — the only thing I believe is certain: Though life is often hard, it is always a blessing. Even in the darkest of times, it is a blessing to be alive.

I am content with my existence now. And I would not want you to think otherwise. Still, I must admit, my thoughts are often more of the past than of the present. My memories are very precious to me. Sometimes at the end of a day I go to sit by myself on a hilltop overlooking the sea. As the sun sets, I look out across the water. I close my eyes. In my mind, I am once more with my beloved Nancy. Together on icy, mysterious seas, we are sailing again, sailing away in our wonderful upside-down ship.

I think perhaps all great adventures are like that. We struggle toward their ending. And then the end comes, and we are left with a longing to go back. We want to relive every moment, somehow hold on to all that is over, all that is lost.

About the Author

Don L. Wulffson teaches English, creative writing, and remedial reading in Los Angeles, California. He is the author of an adult novel, eighteen books for young people, numerous educational programs, and more than three hundred stories, poems, and plays, both adult and juvenile. Mr. Wulffson is a graduate of U.C.L.A. and lives with his wife and two daughters in Northridge, California.